"First of all, don't sit like that." McCade pulled her so that she faced him, so that their knees were almost touching, and he leaned forward slightly. "Step one: Invade the woman's personal space. Step two: Direct eye contact." He smiled into Sandy's eyes.

"McCade, this is silly—"

"I'm not finished. Now, without saying a word, a man can let a woman know he's interested in her." He let his eyes drop, focusing for a moment on her full lips, then lingering on the low neckline of her dress. "That's step number three. And if by now she hasn't run away, he might try step four—a nonsexual touch, something harmless like a handshake . . ." He lifted her hand, drawing her fingers into his. ". . . but turn that handshake into a caress," he continued, running his thumb lightly over the back of her hand.

Sandy stared down at her hand as he continued the sensuous movement. When she met his gaze, she could see the heat in his blue eyes. He moistened his lips with the tip of his tongue and her mouth went dry.

"Or you could try surrogate touching." He used one finger to trace the pattern of the fabric covering her couch. "It sends out a signal that says . . . I'd really rather be touching you. . . ."

WHAT ARE *LOVESWEPT* ROMANCES?

They are stories of true romance and touching emotion. We believe those two very important ingredients are constants in our highly sensual and very believable stories in the LOVE-SWEPT line. Our goal is to give you, the reader, stories of consistently high quality that may sometimes make you laugh, sometimes make you cry, but are always fresh and creative and contain many delightful surprises within their pages.

Most romance fans read an enormous number of books. Those they truly love, they keep. Others may be traded with friends and soon forgotten. We hope that each LOVESWEPT romance will be a treasure—a "keeper." We will always try to publish

LOVE STORIES YOU'LL NEVER FORGET
BY AUTHORS YOU'LL ALWAYS REMEMBER

The Editors

Loveswept 889

BODY LANGUAGE

SUZANNE BROCKMANN

BANTAM BOOKS
NEW YORK · TORONTO · LONDON · SYDNEY · AUCKLAND

BODY LANGUAGE
A Bantam Book / May 1998

ISBN 0-553-44662-2

Published simultaneously in the United States and Canada

Bantam Books are published by Bantam Books, a division of Bantam Doubleday Dell Publishing Group, Inc. Its trademark, consisting of the words "Bantam Books" and the portrayal of a rooster, is Registered in U.S. Patent and Trademark Office and in other countries. Marca Registrada. Bantam Books, 1540 Broadway, New York, New York 10036.

PRINTED IN THE UNITED STATES OF AMERICA

OPM   10 9 8 7 6 5 4 3 2 1

For Melanie & Jason

ONE

The electronic ring of the telephone shrilled through the darkness of the bedroom. The first ring woke Cassandra Kirk from an uneasy sleep. The second ring made her sit up and glare groggily at the glowing red numbers on her clock radio.

Two forty-five.

A phone call at two forty-five could only mean one of three things. Disaster at the studio—maybe this interminable and unseasonable rain had flooded the video archives. Death or injury in the family—maybe her mother who lived in Florida had fallen and broken her hip. Or . . .

She picked up the phone after the third ring. "Hello?"

"Yo, Sandy, did I wake you?" Or maybe Clint Mc-Cade was in another time zone and just wanted to say hi.

With a groan, Sandy pushed her long, blonde hair back from her face. "McCade, it's quarter to three in the *morning*." The line crackled. "Where are you?" she asked. "It sounds like you're calling from the moon."

He laughed. "I'm back in the States," he said. "You up for a visit?" McCade's familiar husky voice was laced with amusement, as always.

"Is it that time of year again?" She lay back in her bed. "Time for the annual misfits of Henderson High reunion?"

"Is that a yes?"

"What would you like, McCade? An engraved invitation? Of course it's a yes. But you know, I've made my second bedroom into an office. You'll have to crash in the living room. The couch pulls out."

"Hey, last week I was sleeping in a tent in the rain forest. Trust me, there's nowhere to go from there but up. Your couch sounds first class."

"What's your ETA?" she asked. "My schedule's pretty heavy at work. I've got meetings all morning, but I can hide the key outside the condo for you—"

"You got a meeting in five minutes?" McCade said.

"What!"

"I'm calling from the U-Tote-Em on the corner." He laughed again. "See you in a few." The line disconnected with a click.

Only Clint McCade would dare to call her in the middle of the night from the convenience store down the block. Only Clint McCade would be gutsy enough to assume that she wouldn't get angry at being woken up, and that she wouldn't mind the inconvenience of an overnight guest with no advance notice.

Sandy rolled over to hang up the phone and turn on the light. Shrugging into her bathrobe, she glanced into the mirror. She looked exhausted, exactly as she should, having been awakened at quarter to three in the morning after suffering for hours with work-related, anxiety-induced insomina. But Clint McCade wouldn't care what she looked like. McCade didn't see her as a woman. She was Sandy to him, his old grade-school buddy, his pal, his best friend.

She went into the kitchen to set her coffeemaker on stun. She knew from past experience that she wasn't going to get any sleep for the next few hours at least. McCade would ask her what she'd been up to in the months since she'd seen him last. Then he'd have to fill her in on *his* latest projects before she came face-to-face with her pillow again. Rain forest. Hadn't he said something about a rain forest? Come to think of it, this could take all night.

Sandy smiled. She loved having McCade around.

It wasn't supposed to rain in Phoenix, Arizona. It was the *desert*, for Pete's sake. But the rain had been following McCade for weeks now, starting when he was down in South America, and continuing even after he hit his current home base of L.A.

So why should he have been surprised that it rained on him nearly his entire trip along Route 10 from L.A. to Phoenix? Hell, with his current record, he could take a trip to the moon and it would rain all the way there.

He pulled his Harley under the protection of the condo complex's carport, next to Sandy's little blue Geo, and cut the motor. Mercy, he was soaked. His black leather jacket was soggy, and his boots squished when he stood up. His bag of clothes was supposedly waterproof, but he doubted anything could have withstood the deluge he'd been through.

Except for the case protecting his video camera. He could sink that camera with the *Titanic*, and the case would stay airtight. Not that it would matter. This camera would operate just as well underwater as above it.

He unlocked the camera case from the back of his bike, and glancing up at the lights blazing in the windows of Sandy's condo, he lugged it and his duffel bag toward the courtyard.

Damn, now that he was here, he was scared to death. What was he going to tell her? That one minute he'd been sitting in his living room in L.A., trying to unwind after a rigorous three-month stint on location as a cameraman on a picture about the rain forests, and the next he'd been screaming down the highway toward Phoenix with only his camera and a couple of changes of underwear and T-shirts stuffed into his duffel bag?

Was he going to tell Sandy that in L.A. his entire life, his entire existence suddenly seemed so plastic and surreal that he'd nearly panicked, unable to remember a single moment in the past year when he had felt happy— sincerely, honestly *felt* happy?

But then he'd remembered the trip he and Sandy had made to the Phoenix Zoo the last time he'd been in town. He'd been happy then. In fact, he had been happy the entire two weeks of his visit. They'd spent two solid days movie marathoning—going to a multiplex theater for the first screening of the day and staying until the place shut down, seeing six different movies in a row, living on a diet of popcorn and soda and ice-cream nuggets. They'd also gone hiking out in the desert, looking for sidewinders and jackrabbits—two kids from the streets of New Jersey versus the wilds of Arizona. They'd laughed so hard it had hurt.

Sandy was his best friend, his confidante, his rock in a world of quicksand.

Beautiful, golden Sandy, with the shy smile and the

purest blue eyes he'd ever seen. Sandy, who was smart, gorgeous, and talented, but totally unable to see it in herself. She had no self-esteem, no idea how special she was. When she looked into the mirror, she still saw the awkward little girl in ill-fitting clothes, the girl who lived on the wrong side of the tracks in a wealthy suburb of New York City, where high-school popularity was directly related to the kind of car daddy could afford to buy his daughter. But Sandy had had no daddy, and her mother couldn't even afford to buy herself a car, let alone one for Sandy.

That little girl had adopted a "to hell with them" attitude and a great sense of humor, but the insecurities had never fully disappeared.

Setting his camera on the floor, he rang the doorbell.

The door swung open, and the warmth and light of Sandy's smile spilled out into the hallway. But the welcome in her eyes quickly turned to disbelief and barely concealed horror.

"Oh, McCade!" She backed away. "You're covered with *mud.*"

He was splattered, from the top of his wet hair to the tips of his black cowboy boots.

"Don't move," she ordered him, taking both the camera and his duffel bag out of his hands and carrying them quickly across the rug to the linoleum floor of her kitchen, where the mud would be easier to clean up.

"Off," she demanded, coming back out and pointing to his muddy attire. "Everything off out here. You are going directly to the shower, do not pass go, do not collect two hundred dollars."

McCade leaned against the door, crossing his arms. "Sandy, old buddy, old pal, you're not *really* going to make me undress out here in the hall, are you?"

"Damn straight I am." She crossed her arms, too, smiling sweetly up at him. "I just had my carpets cleaned, old buddy, old pal."

Her hair was loose around her shoulders, and her face was free of makeup. She looked fresh, scrubbed clean, and much younger than her twenty-seven years. From an artist's point of view, her face was damn close to perfection. It was a near-perfect oval, with a wide, high forehead and well-proportioned cheekbones that took on an almost exotic cast when she smiled. Her nose was neither too big or too small, and her chin and jaw were strong, almost too strong, if one really had to find a fault with her face. Her lips were full, her mouth generous, curving into a smile that revealed her white, perfect teeth. But her eyes . . .

Delicately shaped with an alluring tilt, they were blue gray, and so totally blue gray that they were nearly colorless. Unlike many average pairs of blue eyes, like his own for instance, Sandy's had no flecks of gold or green mixed in. Pure blue gray, with thousands of tiny lightning bolts of white shooting from the pupil toward the edge of the iris. Fabulous. Sandy truly had fabulous eyes.

McCade had searched the world for another pair of eyes like Sandy's but came up empty-handed every time.

There was a questioning look in those eyes now, questioning the length and extent of his scrutiny.

"You look good, Sand," he said with a quick smile as he sat down heavily on the stairs and began pulling off his boots.

"You look like hell," she replied. "What's with the beard, Grizzly?"

It was hard to tell exactly how McCade looked underneath all the mud. His rain-soaked hair hung in dark, stringy strands a good three inches past his shoulders, and the entire lower half of his handsome face was covered by a curly beard and mustache. His nose was definitely McCade's—long and straight and a touch too big, the dominant feature of his face. Until he smiled, that is.

He smiled at her again, his familiar, crooked grin. The beard hid the way his face dimpled up in lines around either side of his mouth, but his teeth seemed even whiter against the darkness of the curly hair. He looked tired, and he had more crow's-feet around his eyes than he'd had the last time she'd seen him. And there was an odd light sparkling in his blue eyes as he looked up at her.

"I was going for that 'back to nature' look down in South America." He shrugged out of his leather jacket.

"You forgot to pack your razor."

He grinned, but didn't deny it. The black T-shirt he was wearing was also soaking wet, and he quickly pulled that over his head.

Muscles. McCade had always had lots of muscles, even back in middle school, where they met when he was in seventh grade and she was in sixth. Sandy had quickly become immune to the sight of his perfectly sculpted body. Even now she could go out in public with McCade and be totally oblivious to the fact that he had a hunk rating of about twenty-five on a scale of one to ten, even while women were hyperventilating and fainting all around them.

Well, maybe she wasn't totally oblivious.

If she were totally oblivious, she wouldn't be standing there, watching him peel his wet jeans off his powerful thighs, suddenly painfully aware that it had been nearly four years since she'd been in a physical relationship with a man.

She smiled to herself. With any luck at all, that was going to change, and soon.

"What's the joke?" McCade asked, wrestling his pants down around his ankles.

"My life," Sandy said. "Shower first, then I'll give you the gory details."

Sandy grinned, imagining what old Mrs. Hobbs across the hall would think if she looked out the peephole in her door right now.

McCade was wearing a pair of teal-colored briefs, and he hooked his thumbs in the white elastic waistband and looked at her. "You sure you want everything off?" he said questioningly, one eyebrow raised.

"No, no, McCade," she said hastily. "Come on in. You're clean. I doubt even *you* could manage to get mud on your underwear."

"Don't wash my leather jacket," he said, disappearing down the hall toward the bathroom.

"Of course, I'm not going to wash your leather jacket," Sandy muttered, shaking her head as she gathered up his dirty clothes. After dropping off his boots and jacket in the kitchen, she put what was left in the washing machine, then went back for the rain-soaked briefs McCade had tossed on the floor in front of the bathroom door. Teal. McCade looked good in teal. He would also look good *not* in teal.

Shame on you, Cassandra Kirk, she scolded herself silently, for thinking such lascivious thoughts about your old pal, McCade. He had made it more than clear for the past fifteen years that they were friends, period. Besides, a man who regularly dated models and actresses would never even look twice at her.

With a sigh, she went into her bedroom to fish in her

closet for her old terrycloth robe. Even though it was pink, it was the largest and least frilly of her bathrobes.

The shower was going full force, and steam escaped from the open bathroom door. Sandy pushed it open even farther, raising her voice so that McCade could hear her over the sound of the running water.

"I'm putting a robe on the back of the door," she said, "and a clean towel on the rack, okay?"

"You know what I could really use?" McCade's husky voice said from behind the shower curtain.

"I'm almost afraid to ask," Sandy muttered. "What?"

McCade pulled the curtain back slightly and looked out at her. The expression he wore on his face was one she had never seen before. His eyes were haunted, hungry, and his lean face unsmiling. He looked predatory. Must be the beard, Sandy thought. But still, something prompted her to ask, "Are you okay, McCade?"

"I could really use a beer," he said, as if he hadn't heard her, then pulled the curtain closed.

Underneath the pummeling water of the shower, McCade closed his eyes, letting the full force of the spray hit his head. Lord have mercy, he was *not* okay. He was a psychological wreck, a total mess, and now that he was here, he couldn't seem to bring himself to tell her why he had come. *You know what I could really use?* he had asked her. But he hadn't answered the way he'd wanted to. You, he'd wanted to say. He should have climbed out of the shower and taken her into his arms. She was probably wearing one of those silly little nightie things underneath her bathrobe.

He groaned, then pulled his mind back to the problem at hand. He was going to have to tell her, he was going to have to just say it. That's why he'd come here, wasn't it?

McCade turned off the water. Plastic rings screeched along the metal rod as he pulled the shower curtain back and grabbed the towel Sandy had laid out for him. He'd dry off, go out into the living room, drink a beer, and gather his courage while listening to Sandy tell him about her current gigs at work. Then he'd take a deep breath and just tell her . . . what? That he needed her? That he wanted her more than he'd ever wanted anyone or anything? That God help him—he was almost one hundred percent certain that he *loved* her?

He wasn't even sure he could say that word aloud.

An open bottle of beer was waiting for him on the coffee table in the living room. Sandy was sitting with her feet curled up underneath her on one end of the comfortable couch. He tightened the belt on the pink bathrobe and sat down next to her.

"The pink goes nicely with the beard," she said. "So tell me, McCade, what have you been up to? Cavorting through rain forests, hmm? Come on, spill."

But he shook his head as he took a long pull from the bottle of beer. "You first."

She turned toward him, her arm up along the back of the couch. "I have just won the most amazing contract." Her eyes sparkled. "You know who Simon Harcourt is?"

McCade studied his beer thoughtfully, frowning slightly. Finally he shook his head. "No, I don't."

"Locally, he's really hot stuff," Sandy said. "Self-made billionaire, supporter of the arts and the environment. He headed an education task force a few years ago that really shook up the system, he started an AIDS awareness program. . . ." She shook her head in awe and respect. "Anyway, to make a long story short, he's running for governor, and I've just clinched a deal with his people. I'm going to be making all of his campaign commercials—right now they want five—along with two docu-bios, a ten-minute and a thirty-minute."

McCade grinned back at her. "That's great, Sand. What's your role? Producer? Director?"

"Both. In fact, I may even do some of the camera work myself."

"I'm between jobs, if you need an extra hand."

Sandy stared at him incredulously. "Are you kidding?" But then she shook her head. "I couldn't even pay you one quarter of what you usually get."

He shrugged. "Pay me union scale. It sounds like fun, and—"

She launched herself at him, throwing her arms around his neck in a friendly hug. Still holding the bottle of beer, McCade wrapped his arms around her, closing his eyes and breathing in the clean scent of her hair. Damn, she was so soft, so warm and sweet. Why had he waited so long to realize that everything he'd ever wanted was right here?

She pulled back slightly to grin at him. "You're hired," she said, then frowned. "It's going to take three or four weeks to get all the footage I'll need."

"I'm not planning on going anywhere." He gazed into her eyes. God, couldn't she feel his heart pounding? He swallowed. He had to say it. "Look, Sand—"

"There's more I have to tell you." She pulled free from his arms and settled back into the couch. She smiled at him, a bewitching mixture of amusement and self-consciousness. "McCade, I'm in love."

McCade stared at her. "Love?"

Sandy nodded, her eyes filled with happiness. "I've finally met the man of my dreams," she said. "Last week.

His name's James Vandenberg. James Austin Vandenberg the Fourth, can you believe it? He's Harcourt's right-hand man. He's got a law degree from Harvard, he's smart and nice and tall, almost as tall as you are. He's outrageously handsome, with this wavy, black hair and brown eyes you could die for. He's single, straight, thirty-three years old, and currently unattached. . . ."

Sandy's words washed over McCade as he continued to stare at her. She was in love. With someone else. He felt sick to his stomach, sick clear through to his soul. His disappointment was laced with a white-hot anger. Dammit, why hadn't he come out here a week ago? Why hadn't he figured out how he'd felt months ago when he was last visiting? He was angry, hurt, and shocked—shocked that the incredible McCade luck had finally seemed to run out. He carefully put the bottle of beer down on the table, amazed that his hand wasn't shaking uncontrollably.

"Is he here?" he asked suddenly, interrupting her.

"What?"

"Is he here, now?"

Understanding made her cheeks flush. "No!"

"Why not?"

"I just met the man last week—"

"If it's really love, Sandy, why are you waiting?"

Sandy pulled her eyes away from McCade's piercing gaze, sat up, slumped back down again, then laughed, a short, nonhumorous-sounding burst of air. She shook her head slightly, pushing her hair away from her face. "If you must know the truth, James doesn't even know I exist, all right? Happy, McCade?"

No. No, he wasn't happy. But why not? Why wasn't he feeling relieved? Sandy wasn't actually involved with this man yet—this smart, nice lawyer with the long, old-money-sounding name. This man was probably a perfect match for her, and no doubt was easier to get along with, easier to live with than McCade would ever be.

"Enough about me and James," she said. "Tell me about the rain forests—"

"Kirk, can I tell you tomorrow?" McCade asked. "I, um . . . I've got to crash, like, right now. I just, you know, hit the exhaustion wall and . . ."

Sandy's eyes widened with surprise. "Yeah, sure." She looked at him closely. "Are you really all right, Mc-Cade? You look a little pale."

"I must be fighting off a bug or something," he lied lamely.

She just looked at him, her beautiful face serious, her eyes sober. "Clint," she said finally, "you'd tell me if you had a real problem, wouldn't you?"

He glanced at her. "Of course. You're my best friend," he said simply. "But really, I'm just . . . tired."

She smiled at him, and McCade made himself smile back, trying to hide the way his heart had fractured into a million pieces.

TWO

McCade had planned to shave his beard when he hit Phoenix. But as he looked into the bathroom mirror in the morning, he couldn't bear the thought of exposing his face—and the expression of utter woe he knew was on it—to the eyes of everyone around him.

Sandy had set an alarm clock that woke him up at ten. It gave him enough time to shower and grab something to eat before the preproduction meeting she had scheduled in her office at eleven-thirty.

As McCade pulled on his slightly stiff jeans he mentally shook his head, amazed at himself. Why wasn't he already long gone?

All morning long he'd been vacillating between his choices. He could (A) hop on his bike and ride out of town as quickly as he rode in. Except he had promised Sandy he'd do that camera work for her. Of course, he hadn't known when he'd made that promise that she had the hots for some other man. . . .

So he could always (B) stay in town and totally sabotage her attempts to catch this lawyer guy's eye, then sweep her off her feet while she was on the rebound. Or he could (C) act the part of the good old best friend and help her out.

He could help her get noticed by a nice, wealthy man who would be able to give her the kind of life she had always wanted—the upper-class, country-club kind of life. The kind of life McCade could never give her, no matter how much money he had in the bank.

Sure, he could buy his way into a country club, God forbid he should ever even *want* to. And therein lay the problem. Sandy had always wanted the culture, the re-finement, the *recognition* that came with wealth. McCade didn't. He could afford the finest wine any vineyard in the world could offer, but frankly, he didn't like the stuff. He'd drink beer or water, thanks a lot.

What it all boiled down to was, McCade was content to be McCade. He had a job he liked, comfortable clothes he liked to wear, and the fact that he had close to a half a million dollars in his bank account wasn't going to change anything except maybe the brand of beer he bought and the places he visited on vacation. Sure, he liked to live comfortably without the threat of eviction hanging over his head the way it once had. Sure, he liked to have money to spend on movies and music and what-ever whim came floating in on the wind. But he saw no need to wear his wealth like a badge, hell, he flat out didn't want to. And last time he checked, black leather jackets weren't welcome at the local country club.

But that was the life Sandy wanted.

In the kitchen, McCade's boots and jacket were still damp. He pulled the boots on anyway and took his sun-glasses out of his jacket pocket.

The hot Arizona wind dried his long hair as he slowly rode his Harley down Indian School Road east toward Scottsdale, toward Forty-fourth Street, where Sandy's video production house was. It was April in Phoenix, and the roads and sidewalks were sizzling with heat. It had to be damn near ninety degrees in the shade. And it wasn't even summer yet.

As McCade pulled into the parking lot of Video Enterprises, Inc., he came to a nondecision of sorts. He had to wait and see exactly what this James Austin Whoziwhatsis the Fourteenth was like before he gave him the thumbs-up or -down. Besides, if he was going to bolt, he had to think up a good explanation to give Sandy. By now she was probably counting on his camera work for her campaign project.

He opened the front doors of the office building and stepped into the air-conditioned darkness of the lobby. As he took the elevator up to the second floor, he took off his sunglasses, hanging them casually by one earpiece over the neck of his black T-shirt.

The elevator door opened and McCade stared directly at his reflection in the big mirror that hung on the wall. He almost didn't recognize himself. His long hair and beard, combined with his imposing height and muscles, made him look like a bouncer at a biker bar, or a patron who would probably need to be bounced.

McCade walked down the hall to the main conference room—the briefing room, he liked to call it. It was a large airy room with big windows that looked out over the desert-landscaped front yard of the building. A big oval table sat in the middle of a soothing, earth-toned carpet, surrounded by more than a dozen comfortable chairs.

"Can I help you?" Sandy's assistant, Frank Williamson, intercepted McCade almost before he was in the room.

"Yo, Frank," McCade said, and behind his glasses, the younger man's eyes widened in surprise.

"McCade, my God, this may come as a shock to you, but you're covered with hair."

McCade grinned. "It's the new me. Whaddaya think?"

Frank crossed his arms and studied McCade. "I think for a guy who usually has chicks fainting in the street, you look like hell," he finally said. "What's up? Was your last gig on a desert island?"

McCade crossed his own arms. "Frank. When someone says 'what do you think?' they don't *really* want to know what you think. Ever hear of something called 'tact?'"

"Tact is for little old ladies who've just had their hair done," Frank told him. "Not for a guy like you who could stand in as a body double for Arnold Schwarzenegger"—he lowered his voice—"you know, the boss hasn't gone out on a single date since you were here last."

Both men turned and looked across the room, to where Sandy was standing by the windows, talking to a man who had to be James.

McCade's heart sank as he took in the expensive cut and fabric of the man's obviously hand-tailored suit. It sank even further as he studied the way James filled his suit. He was a tall man, just a little bit shorter than McCade's own six feet three inches, and he was built like McCade—strong, broad shoulders, narrow waist, slim hips. James turned slightly, and McCade caught a glimpse of the man's face. His features were chiseled and handsome, his nose long and aristocratic. His chin was strong and his lips almost too femininely shaped. Almost, but not quite.

Damn. With his wavy black hair cut conservatively short and his dark eyes, this guy's picture should have been in the dictionary under *dreamboat*.

"How you can keep a relationship platonic with someone like the boss is one of the last great mysteries of the world, McCade." Frank glanced down at his clipboard, then up at the clock. "Grab a seat, pal, we're gonna get started."

McCade crossed to the conference table and slid into the chair immediately to the left of the seat at the head of the table, where he knew Sandy would sit.

He watched her talk to James. Her shoulders were tense, and her body was tight. She didn't seem to be able to look the man directly in the eye. Boy, she was nervous. Her hands fluttered about, then grabbed onto the files she was holding as if they were a lifeline.

As McCade watched she glanced at her watch and said something to James with a weak smile. It was an approximation of her usual five-hundred-watt grin. McCade shook his head. Unless she relaxed, this guy was only going to see a high-strung, stressed-out, rough imitation of Sandy. And with her hair wrapped tight in a bun, wearing that much-too-conservative navy jacket and skirt, she wasn't winning any points appearance-wise either. It's not that she wasn't pretty, he quickly corrected himself. She was. She just wasn't as earthshakingly beautiful as he knew she could be.

She spotted him sitting at the table, and her smile instantly turned warmer.

"Gee, and I went to all that trouble to find a new razor to leave out on the sink for you this morning," she said in a low voice as she sat down next to him.

McCade fingered his beard. "I'm thinking about

growing it really long." He smiled. "You know, like the guys in ZZ Top?"

But her attention was instantly gone as James sat down on her immediate right, directly across the table from McCade.

Hell, the man was even better looking close up. As McCade looked at James the dark-haired man met his gaze. For a brief instant McCade could see a flash of disapproval, or maybe it was disdain in the man's dark eyes, accompanied by a heaping serving of mistrust.

It was a look that was unmistakable, and it said loud and clear that James didn't trust anyone who looked the way McCade did.

Small-minded, thought McCade.

James Vandenberg IV was clearly no different from those high-school kids who had snubbed Sandy and McCade all those years ago because of the way they looked, because they couldn't afford designer jeans and expensive clothes.

Didn't Sandy see that? But then it occurred to him—despite the rotten treatment they'd received, Sandy had always secretly yearned for acceptance from the elite cliques in school. By winning James's attention and heart, she'd be achieving what she'd always wanted.

She'd been waiting for a guy like James for all of her life.

The wave of jealousy that hit McCade nearly took his breath away.

He grabbed onto the copies of the shooting schedule that Sandy had just passed around.

McCade did his best to ignore James as he studied the information silently. Sandy had booked him as her floating camera, her creative lens for every single event. Carrying a handheld, he wouldn't be tied down to any one location; he could take reaction shots, or shoot from interesting angles. It was his favorite job on a project like this, and she knew it. It was obvious that she cared about him—just not in the right way.

He took a deep breath and read that the first shoot was scheduled for Saturday night. It was an election fund-raiser, a dinner dance up at the Pointe, one of Phoenix's poshest resorts. Harcourt would be making a speech that Sandy wanted taped for soundbite pirating.

"If there are any questions or problems during the shoots, and both Frank and I are unavailable," Sandy was saying, "Mr. Vandenberg is the man to talk to."

"James," he corrected her with a charming smile. But he glanced toward McCade with a look that seemed to say, *Mister* Vandenberg to anyone who looks like *you.*

"Okay, we're set, then," Sandy said, ending the meeting. "See you all on Saturday."

Sandy sat for a moment as the room cleared, organizing her files before putting them back in her briefcase. McCade still sat on her left, obviously not going anywhere. With his hair parted in the middle and hanging down around his shoulders, and his thick, curly beard, he looked faintly biblical, as if he were one of the Apostles in the painting of the Last Supper. Except for the miniature dragon tattooed on his right biceps, she thought with a smile. Somehow she doubted that any of Jesus's twelve had had a tattoo.

"Okay, I think I've got everything I need," James interrupted her thoughts. "I'll see you Saturday evening. The schedule says you'll be setting up at five?"

"We'll be there." Sandy smiled back at him.

"Oh, I almost forgot." James reached into his inside jacket pocket and took out a small envelope. "Mr. Harcourt asked me to give you comp tickets for the dinner dance that follows Saturday's speech."

"Oh, I don't know." Sandy bit her lip. "I'm not really—"

"She'll take 'em, thanks." McCade snatched the envelope deftly from James's hand and tucked the tickets inside her briefcase.

"McCade is an old high-school friend of mine," Sandy told James. "*And* he happens to be the best cameraman both in and outside of Hollywood. We're lucky to have him working with us on this project."

McCade could see James reappraising him as they shook hands.

"Nice to meet you." James's dark eyes were much warmer than they'd been when he'd examined McCade across the table during the meeting.

The man had a ton and a half of charisma and charm. And he could turn it off and on like a faucet.

"See you both on Saturday." With another quick smile at Sandy, he was gone.

Sandy met McCade's gaze and smiled wryly. "Ouch," she said. "I'm in pain."

McCade was too.

"So whaddaya think?" she asked, closing the conference-room door to ensure their privacy.

He sat on the edge of the table, crossing his arms in front of him. "He seems kind of . . ." Phony? Plastic? Serious? Un-fun? All of those words seemed appropriate, but he didn't dare utter a single one aloud. Instead he shrugged.

Sandy laughed, crossing her own arms. "McCade, you have such a gift with words."

"I'm into the visual. Give me a break."

"Did you think . . ." she started to say, then hesitated. "Do you think he even knows I exist?"

McCade looked down at the floor, then glanced back up at her. "Honestly?"

"No, lie to me, McCade," she said tartly. "Of *course* honestly, you idiot—"

"If you want him to notice you, you're going to have to work a little harder."

"I guess I should just forget it—"

"Will you please stop selling yourself short?"

Sandy took two big steps backward, startled by his anger and the sheer volume of his voice.

"You're a gorgeous, intelligent, funny, sexy, damned *incredibly* desirable woman," McCade fumed, "and a jerk like James Vandenberg should thank his lucky stars that you'd even give him the time of day. If you want him— Do you want him?"

Sandy closed her mouth and nodded.

"Fine," McCade said grimly. "You'll get him. Starting Saturday, he's going to notice you, big time."

Grabbing her arm, he pulled her toward the door. She barely had time to snatch her briefcase from the conference-room table before he was yanking her down the hallway toward the elevators.

"Where are we going?" she asked.

"You're taking the afternoon off."

"I can't just—"

"Yes," McCade said firmly. "You can."

Sandy sat looking in the mirror as McCade's friend Tony attacked her hair with a pair of scissors. "But I don't *want* a perm," she said belligerently. "I had one once, remember, McCade? I looked like I stuck my finger in a socket. It was frizz city for *months.*"

"Did *I* give you that perm, babycakes?" Tony asked. The snipping sounds of his scissors stopped as he met her eyes in the mirror. He was a huge bear of a man, almost as wide around as he was tall. He wore a pale green surgical scrub shirt over baggy white pants and sandals.

The cool colors of his clothes fit in with the Art Deco decor of the beauty parlor. The walls were melon, trimmed with a light shade of aqua. The shiny counters matched the trim. Everything was so clean, it glistened.

"*Did* I?" Tony asked again.

"No," she said slowly.

"Well, there you go." He gave her an angelic smile and resumed cutting.

Sandy looked at McCade, who was leaning against the counter, his arms folded across his chest.

"What if I hate it?" she asked.

"You won't," Tony promised. "Sweet pea, I can guarantee that."

McCade had met Tony in Hollywood on a movie set. He'd told Sandy that quite a number of famous women had put their trademark tresses into Tony's able hands and he'd never let a single one of them down. Tony had moved to Scottsdale because of his asthma, and many of his Hollywood clients chose to make the short commuter flight to Arizona rather than take their chances with another hairdresser in L.A.

"McCade, you're next in line for my chair," Tony told him. "The Robinson Crusoe look is definitely passé, darling."

"Not today, Tony," McCade replied. "There's not enough time."

"It'll take all of fifteen minutes," Tony said. "While Sandy's perm is setting."

"But I haven't agreed—" Sandy started.

"No, I'm going shopping," McCade interrupted. "I'm going to update Sandy's wardrobe."

Sandy started to laugh. "You? You're going to buy me new *clothes?*"

His smile held a trace of grimness. "I know what men like."

"That's what I'm afraid of."

"Have the perm. I'll be back to pick you up . . . When, Tony?"

"Two hours."

"In two hours," McCade said.

"You don't even know what size I am," Sandy protested.

"You wear a nine," he said. "Size-eight shoes. Bra size, thirty-four-B—"

"Well, jeez, McCade," Sandy sputtered. "Announce it to everyone, why don't you? I think there're a couple of ladies with their heads under the hair dryers who didn't hear you!"

But she was talking to his back as he walked out the door, lifting one hand in a farewell wave.

"Are we ready for our perm?" Tony asked, a smile on his cherubic face.

"You really think it'll look okay?" she asked him.

Tony's smile got bigger. "Sweetness, okay is not the word for what I have in mind." He lifted up her long straight hair. "Just picture it. Soft, wavy curls around your face. Your hair will have body, life. One toss of your head will drive McCade wild. He won't be able to keep his hands off of you. And *that's* a promise."

"McCade and I are just friends," Sandy said.

"Of course you are." Tony's patronizing smile said he didn't believe it.

Sandy shook her head with a laugh. "Do it," she heard herself say. "Let's do it."

McCade piled the last of the shopping bags into the trunk of Sandy's car and headed back to Tony's. He was in a bad mood, and it had probably been his last stop that did him in. He'd gone into the mall's lingerie store, and the thought that he was picking out fancy under-things that he'd probably never see on Sandy depressed him. The thought that James Vandenberg probably *would* see the richly colored silks and lace against her soft skin made him crazy.

Why the hell was he doing this?

Because he loved Sandy. Because he wanted her to be happy. Because a part of him was still hoping that she'd turn around, throw her arms around him, and declare that she couldn't possibly love James, it was McCade who owned her heart.

Right. Dream on, McCade.

He pulled open the door to Tony's little shop. The wave of cool air hit him the moment that he saw her, and it was a good thing, or he might have passed out from the heat that engulfed him.

Sandy's hair was parted on the side, swept up and over, curling and loose around her beautiful face. It cascaded around her shoulders and down her back, the curls catching and reflecting the light, seeming to glimmer and shine. Man, she had so much hair. The gentle perm had given it body, lifting its heavy weight from her neck.

She was eating an ice-cream bar, an orange and vanilla Creamsicle, as she sat up on the counter, talking to

Tony and his next customer. McCade watched, spellbound, as her pink tongue caught a drip from the bottom of the ice cream. At that moment she looked up and her eyes met his.

McCade had to look away for fear of spontaneous combustion. He took a deep breath as he walked toward her and actually managed to smile. "You look great. Can I say I told you so?"

"No." She'd returned her attention to her ice cream. "You may not."

Tony's customer was an elderly lady with heavily painted eyebrows and thin white hair that was wet and flattened against her head. She looked in the mirror from Sandy to McCade and back again.

"Your gentleman friend needs a haircut," she said. "And a shave."

"He can be pretty childish when it comes to his hair," Sandy told her as if McCade weren't standing in front of her.

"Underneath it all, he's not half bad looking," the woman decided, "but I really don't think he's your type, dear." She leaned closer to Sandy and lowered her voice as if McCade wouldn't be able to hear her. "His kind's not good enough for a nice young lady like you."

From the circling motions Tony was making with his hand behind the woman's head, it was obvious that he was implying she was as crazy as they came, but still her words stung. McCade turned away, not wanting Sandy to see the hurt in his eyes.

"Oh, but you're wrong," he heard her say earnestly. "Men like Clint McCade are few and far between. In fact, it's taken me fifteen years to find a man who doesn't totally pale in comparison."

McCade's mouth twisted in a wry smile as he shook

his head. Good old Sandy. Loyal to the bitter end. "Come on, Kirk. Let's blow this Popsicle stand. Tony, I owe you one."

"No, no, babycakes." Tony turned as they headed for the door. "I owed *you* one, remember? Now we're even."

As they walked out of the salon McCade ran his fingers through Sandy's new curls so lightly that she didn't even notice.

"McCade." Tony's voice stopped him and he turned back, letting the door close. "She's a nice girl."

"I know." McCade watched out the window as she climbed into her car.

"She says you're just friends."

"That's right."

Tony laughed. "Yeah, and my mother's the pope."

McCade tossed his armload of shopping bags on Sandy's big double bed, then looked up at her and grinned. "I'll go get the rest."

"There's more?" But he was already gone.

Shaking her head, she opened one garment bag first, and then another, pulling out a collection of evening wear, mostly dresses. As she looked at the clothing lying on her bed, she realized her mouth was hanging open, and she closed it. Then she started to laugh.

Never, ever, not in a million years would she have bought any of these dresses for herself. It wasn't that they were ugly or garish; in fact they were all rather simply elegant—no sequins or flashing lights attached, anyway. It was just that she always went for the quietly modest dresses, the ones that would let her blend in with the crowd. But that was the problem. All too often she blended in. Sandy looked at the dresses again. Not anymore. Not a chance.

She opened the other bags to find shoes—all simple high-heeled pumps in various colors to match the dresses.

Then she opened the bag of lingerie and shut it very quickly. She opened it more slowly, reaching in and pulling out something very tiny made of black silk.

McCade came into the room, and she dangled the tiny black thing from her finger. "You don't *really* expect me to wear this, do you, McCade?"

"I wouldn't have bought it if I didn't expect you to wear it." He sat down next to her on the bed. "I think you should wear the white dress on Saturday."

As Sandy watched he began opening one of the last bags he'd brought in from the car. Makeup. He'd bought new eye shadow and blush, and lipstick and . . .

"Go on, why don't you try it on?" He glanced up at her impatiently, as if he expected her to be already changing into the new white dress.

"McCade . . . "

"You want to get noticed, right?"

She nodded. Slowly, though. Reluctantly.

"Look, Kirk, just put on that dress. If you hate it, no one's going to make you wear it."

"Damn right," she muttered. But she picked up the white dress. The fabric was soft, the dress obviously well made. She'd never dared even to try on anything like it before. It would cling to her body, hug her every curve, draw attention to her.

But that was the point, wasn't it? She caught a glimpse of her shiny new curls in the bedroom mirror, and suddenly wanted to see just what she'd look like wearing this dress.

McCade settled back on the bed, obviously not going anywhere, so she took the dress and headed for the door.

"Sandy."

She turned back to see his smile. "Don't forget this." He opened the lingerie bag and tossed something white and impossibly tiny at her.

Sandy changed slowly in the little room she'd made into her home office. There was no mirror, so she couldn't really see what she looked like. But she looked down at the taut white material covering her hips and stomach. The dress *felt* good. And, God! Somehow the design of the bra McCade had bought gave her cleavage. Actual, honest-to-God cleavage!

There was a soft tap on the door. "It's the leg police. You forgot your stockings and shoes."

She pulled the door open, and he stood there, shimmering hose hanging from one hand, a pair of white pumps with very high, lethal-looking spike heels hanging from the other. His eyes traveled slowly and appreciatively down and then back up her body. Sandy folded her arms protectively across her chest.

"Wow. You look—"

She took the stockings and the shoes and closed the door in his face.

The stockings were the sheerest she'd ever encountered. She rolled them slowly up one leg and then the other. She slipped the shoes on her feet, refusing to think about Cinderella. But the white pumps fit perfectly, comfortably, even if they pushed her height over the six-foot mark.

Sandy opened the door to find McCade still waiting for her. He grabbed her by the hand and pulled her down the hall to the kitchen.

"McCade, wait," she complained. "I haven't even seen myself in the mirror yet and—"

He pushed her into one of the kitchen chairs.

"—I haven't learned to walk in these shoes yet and—"

He'd spread all the new makeup he'd bought out on the kitchen table. With a flourish, he drew one of her spare bedsheets around her, covering her completely from the neck down.

"White dress," he explained. "Don't want to get any makeup on it."

"McCade—" Sandy stopped. She took a deep breath and started again, trying to sound rational and in control. "Clint, what are you doing?"

He was looking at her critically in the bright overhead light. "I'm going to put some makeup on you," he told her almost absently as he studied her face. He smiled then, meeting her eyes. "You don't really need much, you look good without it. I'll just enhance what you've already got."

"*You're* going to—"

"I've doubled as makeup assistant on quite a few low-budget projects. Off the record, of course, and only on nonunion jobs." His smile became quite immodest. In fact it was downright smug. "Jim Fabrizio, who is *the* makeup man in Hollywood—"

"I *know* who Fabrizio is," Sandy said.

"He said if I ever wanted to give up camera work, I could have a full-time job working with him."

"Well, you're quite the little bundle of talent, aren't you, McCade?"

"Tip your head back and close your eyes," he commanded. "*And* your mouth, smart aleck."

Sandy obeyed, and she felt him touch her face as he

spread a light coat of base over her skin. For such a big man, his touch was remarkably light, incredibly gentle. She opened her eyes to see his face inches from hers, his eyes intense. He was standing almost on top of her, his long jean-clad legs straddling her own. He shifted his weight slightly and her crossed legs came into contact with the inside of his thigh. But he didn't pull back, and there was nowhere *she* could go.

So she closed her eyes again, trying to relax. His voice was soothing as he softly explained what he was doing, or asked her to move her head a certain way. His breath was hot and sweet against her face.

"Okay," he said finally as he pulled the sheet off of her. "Just one more thing, keep your head back—"

But Sandy's eyes flew open as she felt his hand dip down between her breasts. *"McCade!"*

He was half kneeling, half squatting on the floor in front of her, most of his lower body pressed against her legs as he reached across her. "Chill, Kirk," he ordered her as he rubbed a soft line of makeup between her breasts. "This is an old Hollywood trick. It'll really show off your décolletage."

Sandy tried to ignore the effect his hands were having on her body. She tried to ignore her sudden awareness of every solid inch of McCade that was pressing into her ankles and calves. "Hah," she said, trying desperately to pick a fight with him. If they were fighting, then she wouldn't be tempted to reach out and pull his mouth toward hers. Oh, God, she wasn't actually thinking about *kissing* him, was she?

"Hah," she said again, even more desperately. "Proof. McCade you've finally given me proof. All these years you've denied my claim that I'm built like a boy, but now you've as much as admitted it."

"No way." He put his hand under her chin, making her meet his gaze. "I think you're perfect, Sandy, and don't you forget it."

She stared at him, trapped by the smoky vehemence in his eyes. He was still mere inches away from her, and she could see tiny flecks of brown and green mixed in with the almost aquamarine blue. His pupils were surrounded by a tiny ring of gold. "You have beautiful eyes, McCade," she breathed, and as she watched, his pupils dilated.

This was where he would kiss her, if he were anyone in the world besides Clint McCade.

Instead, he blinked, laughed, and straightened up. "Come here," he commanded.

Sandy tried not to wobble in the precariously high heels as she followed him down the hall. He stepped back when he reached her bedroom door, gesturing grandly for her to go in ahead of him.

She took three steps into the room, then stopped as she caught sight of herself in the big full-length mirror that was on the closet door.

"Oh, my God." Sandy slowly walked toward her reflection. She was . . . beautiful. The white dress fit her snugly, making her figure look slender and feminine instead of skinny, the way she usually thought of herself. The skirt was short and it made her long, slim legs look as if they went on forever. And she had to admit, the shoes *were* pretty damn sexy. Her hair was an explosion of gold and light around her face and down her back. And her face! Her eyes looked exotic, her lashes full and dark, her lips the perfect shade of red for her complexion. Sandy's gaze dropped lower, to the low-cut top of the dress. By God, would you look at that? The tops of her breasts looked lush and full.

She could see McCade in the mirror as he leaned against the door frame, his arms across his chest.

"McCade, you're a magician." She turned to look at him. "A miracle worker."

He shook his head. "Hey, I just knew the right kind of wrapping to put on the package."

She looked at herself again. As the shock was wearing off, reality was setting in. She frowned slightly. "I just . . . don't think I can wear this."

McCade straightened up. "Why not?"

"Well . . ." She searched for a reason. "For one thing, I'm too tall in these shoes."

"Oh, come on, Kirk—"

"No, really, McCade. Look at me. I'm six feet tall."

"Six *gorgeous* feet tall," he countered. "So what?"

"I'll tower over everybody."

"You won't tower over James." Three big steps brought him close to Sandy. "He's as tall as I am, right?"

"A little shorter."

"Only a little." He pulled her into his arms, as if they were going to dance together. He held her tightly, intimately against his lean, strong body. "See, you'll fit him perfectly. He'll love it, he won't have to bend so far to kiss you."

McCade looked down at the woman in his arms. Mercy, he'd been dying to hold Sandy like this for hours. She was staring up at him as if he'd gone crazy, her eyes wide, her soft lips parted in surprise. Oh, man, she felt so good, so heavenly against him. He ran his fingers through her silky hair, wanting her so badly—

He pushed her away from him and jammed his hands in the front pockets of his jeans, praying that she hadn't noticed his growing arousal. Dammit! Somehow he mustered up a grin and managed to meet her eye.

"You're gonna knock his socks off, Kirk. Trust me on that one."

She brought her gaze to the mirror, but quickly looked away. "I still can't wear this on Saturday," she told him, regret in her voice.

"No." McCade crossed his arms again. "You're being negative. Start thinking positively—"

"It would be different if I had a date. But the thought of walking into that room, dressed like this, all by myself . . ." She made a face. "Eeek, you know? I wouldn't know what to do with my hands." She snuck another look back into the mirror. "Or, God, my legs."

"I'll be your date."

"In your leather jacket and jeans? It might work in L.A., McCade, but this is *Phoenix.*"

"No, really." The more McCade thought about it, the more he liked the idea. He'd take her to this stuffed-shirt shindig. It would give him a chance to dance with her, hold her in his arms. "If you show up with a date, that'll make you even more appealing to old James. You know how it is, everybody always wants to play with the other kid's toys."

"Well, jeez, McCade, how can I resist when you put it like *that,*" she said sarcastically as she sat down on the edge of her bed.

"You know what I mean."

She looked up at him, tapping her foot. "You'll have to shave."

"No problem."

"And get your hair cut."

McCade raked his fingers through his hair. "I like my hair this way. Long hair is in style—"

"Not among the country-club set in Phoenix, it's

not." She looked down at her fingernails, pretending to examine a chip in her nail polish.

He watched her for several long moments. He wanted to go. He really wanted to go. Maybe James Vandenberg was seeing someone else. Maybe he didn't like blondes. Maybe if Vandenberg was out of the picture . . .

"All right," he said. "For you, I'll get my hair cut."

Sandy stood up, grinning. "And I get to pick out your clothes, the same way you picked out these for me."

"Fine, but I really don't think you're going to have much of a choice," he told her. "The dinner dance is black tie."

"Yeah, but when they say black, they don't mean leather, McCade."

Maybe Sandy would dance with McCade and realize she didn't want to be with anyone else. Maybe . . .

McCade laughed, and this time he felt his smile reach his eyes.

THREE

McCade sat in the chair with his eyes closed, listening to the hum of the blow-dryer, letting Tony work his magic. He'd awakened late that morning, and had gone into the bathroom to cut and then shave off his beard.

After Tony finished making him look more presentable to the Phoenix socialites he'd be rubbing elbows with this evening, McCade had to swing by and pick up the tuxedo Sandy had picked out and he'd bought for the occasion. She'd talked him into getting a stack of other clothes as well—chinos and polo shirts he swore he'd never wear. The tux wasn't quite his style either, but he didn't have any choice tonight. The alterations were supposed to be done by three-thirty, which would give him barely enough time to get to the condo, change, bully Sandy into her new clothes, and put on her makeup.

He smiled. He liked putting makeup on Sandy. He liked standing close enough to feel her body heat. He liked touching her soft, smooth skin—

"Jeez Louise, you haven't even seen how beautiful

I've made you, and you're already as happy as a little clam." Tony's voice cut into his thoughts. "Or maybe it's thinking about a certain gorgeous blonde that's making you smile."

McCade's eyes opened slowly, and the look he gave Tony was lethal. The hairdresser turned off the dryer, cheerfully ignoring him. "I'd recognize that foolish little smile anywhere, although I must admit I never thought I'd see it on *you*, sweetheart."

"Spare me the analysis," McCade sat forward. "Am I done?"

"Not so fast!" Tony pushed McCade back in his seat. "Don't you go running out of here spreading pieces of your former hair all the way to the door just because I've figured out your terrible secret."

McCade frowned at himself in the mirror. His wavy brown hair looked . . . upwardly mobile. Shorter on the sides and around his ears, moussed up and off his forehead in the front, yet long enough to flop down when gravity or humidity won the ongoing battle. With the sun streaks of blond, he looked like he spent his weekends sailing or, ugh, even playing golf.

"I notice you're not denying anything." Tony slowly gathered up the big bib that had caught most of McCade's cut hair.

"That's because I'm ignoring you," McCade said calmly.

"Deny it." The hairdresser's brown eyes were suddenly serious. "Look me in the eye and say, 'Tony, I am not in love with Sandy.' "

McCade met Tony's steady gaze. "Tony, I am not in love with—" But he had to look away. "Dammit."

Tony knew better than to tease. He crossed his big arms over his ample girth. "McCade, if you love this girl, why the *hell* are you helping her catch some other guy?"

"I want her to be happy," he said simply.

Tony erupted in a fit of laughter. "You want her to be happy," he wheezed. "Beautiful, just beautiful. Good grief, McCade, I had no idea you were such a flaming idiot. Hasn't it occurred to you that Sandy would be stupendously happy if you told her that you loved her?"

"She doesn't want me," McCade said tightly.

Tony just laughed harder at that. "Tell her you love her, McCade. Or *I* will."

Sandy answered the phone on the first ring. "Hello?"

"It's me."

"McCade, thank God. I was worried about you."

"I told you last night I scheduled an appointment with Tony to get my hair cut and . . ." McCade cleared his throat. "He, uh, didn't call you, did he?"

"Tony? Why would he call *me?*"

"I don't know. Look, I'm really running late."

"Late I can handle," Sandy told him. "You were gone so long I was starting to think . . ."

"What?"

"Nothing."

"You were starting to think what?"

"Forget it."

"What? That I skipped town?"

"Well, yeah," she admitted. He had been gone when she woke up, and he'd taken his Harley rather than her car. At first she'd thought nothing of it, but as it got later and later she'd started assuming the worst.

"Thanks a lot." All humor was gone from his voice.

"Tell me, when was the last time I promised you something, then didn't deliver?"

"Never. But you've been acting so strangely, I thought maybe—"

"Yeah, well, you were wrong," he said tightly. "Look, they're finishing up the alterations on my tux. I'm going to change here, then get over there as quickly as I can. But it'll be another twenty minutes at least—"

"I'm going to have to meet you up at the Pointe," Sandy cut him off. "I need to get there early. Sorry, but I can't wait for you, McCade."

He swore softly. "I wanted to help you with your makeup."

"I'll have to muddle through on my own," she said. "I'll see you over there, all right?"

"Sandy, wear the white dress, okay?"

"I've already got it on."

"You do?" McCade's good humor was restored. "Way to go! I thought I'd have to dress you myself."

Sandy flushed at the vivid picture that brought to mind. "I've got to get going. Try not to be late."

"You may not recognize me with my hair this short," he told her. "I'll be the one in the tux—holding a camera."

Sandy had never seen so many tuxedos in her life.

The early-evening temperature had to be pushing one hundred degrees Fahrenheit, and tuxedo-clad men quickly crossed the hot pavement between their air-conditioned luxury cars and the cool lobby of the fancy Phoenix resort.

And even greater than the number of tuxedos were the number of sequins in the lobby. Most of the evening gowns that accompanied all those tuxedos were bespattered with sequins and glitter and shiny beads of one kind or another.

Glancing down at her own nonreflective dress, Sandy had to smile. Compared with most of the others, this dress that she had worried so much about wearing was simple and elegantly understated. Short as all get-out, she'd have to admit, but nowhere near as attention seeking as, say, the dress covered with imitation peacock feathers that just walked in the door.

Sandy spotted James Vandenberg near the entrance to the room they would be using for Harcourt's speech. He looked good in a tuxedo. His dark hair was slicked back from his handsome face, and his eyes glistened from the excitement and anticipation that seemed to boil throughout the lobby.

Her stomach clenched with nervousness as she tried to imagine carrying on a conversation with James. She could handle the business end, but after they finished discussing scheduling and camera work, she wouldn't know what to say. She was lousy at small talk, and she had absolutely no idea what the man was interested in. No idea at all.

As she watched, another man in a tuxedo shook hands with James. Sandy slowed her steps. God, didn't it figure that all the men who looked like Greek gods would know each other? The second man had his back to her, but the expensive fabric of his tuxedo looked as if it had been cut and sewn with his body in mind. And what a body. Taller than James, this man was lean and strong, with shoulders that were almost as broad as . . .

No, it couldn't be.

Just then, James turned to survey the crowd and

caught her gaze. His eyes widened slightly and then he smiled. With his eyes still on her, James said something to the man standing next to him.

That man turned around, hoisting a handheld video camera onto his shoulder.

It *was* McCade.

But oh, my God, *what* a McCade! Sandy felt her pulse kick into triple time as her mouth went dry. She had never seen him with his hair this short, she realized. She'd never seen his ears before, at least not for any length of time. He had really nice ears. He had really nice everything. Without the beard, he somehow looked more familiar, yet still so different. It had to be the hair, Sandy decided. The way he was wearing it pushed up and back, so much more of his face could be seen.

McCade was outrageously handsome when half of his face was hidden by his hair. With his whole face showing, he was beyond description.

As Sandy met his gaze a smile curled around the edges of McCade's mouth. His eyes looked like liquid turquoise.

"Hi," she said, her voice sounding breathless.

"Hi," he echoed her. He turned and Sandy followed his gaze, looking straight at James.

James! Oops, he was standing next to her. "Good evening." She took the hand he offered and shook it. "Ready for this?"

"Absolutely," James told her with a flash of his even white teeth. "You look terrific."

He was still holding on to her fingers. "Thank you." She awkwardly pulled her hand free. From the corner of her eyes, she saw McCade fade into the crowd. He was deserting her! No, he was giving her privacy, she realized. But she didn't want privacy. She wanted McCade's quick mind and dry wit near her, ready to take a faltering conversation and revive it.

From across the room, McCade watched as Sandy talked to James. She was tense—her shoulders tight. Her entire body seemed to close in on itself, turning her into a giant bundle of anxiety.

She needed more help. It was going to take more than clothes and a new hairstyle to get Vandenberg's attention. Sandy needed a major attitude adjustment.

As McCade watched she said something and James laughed. But it wasn't a real, honest-to-goodness belly laugh; it was much too polite. They shook hands again and went off in different directions.

McCade pushed his way through the crowd, following Sandy into the conference room where Harcourt was slated to give his speech. But there was no time to talk. She was kept busy right up until the candidate began talking, and then McCade had his job to do. It wasn't until his camera was packed and in one of the equipment vans that he could focus on Sandy.

She was standing by the main door, talking to James and her assistant, Frank. Frank left with a cheery wave, and as McCade watched, Sandy got even more tense. After about thirty more seconds James disappeared.

"Hey." McCade came up behind her. "The band's starting to play in the ballroom. What do you say we take a spin around the floor?"

"Since when do you know how to dance?" Sandy raised one eyebrow. "It's not something you can pick up simply from watching Fred Astaire movies."

"My mother taught me," he admitted.

She laughed. "You're kidding."

"She told me good looks weren't everything. She

said there were three things a man needed to learn in life in order to succeed. One was ballroom dancing."

He pulled her hand into the crook of his arm and led her back toward the ballroom.

"What were the other two?" she asked.

"Research," McCade told her. "She said memorizing the answers to a test didn't make a man smart—it made him a parrot. But a man who knew how to do research had the answers to virtually any question at his fingertips."

A twenty-piece swing band was playing in one corner of the room. McCade tugged Sandy gently toward the dance floor.

"You might know how to dance, but *I* don't."

"Just follow me," he said. "How'd it go with Vandenberg?"

"He makes me really nervous," Sandy admitted.

"So I noticed."

"I made a joke, and I don't think he got it. I wish . . ."

"What?" McCade looked down into her eyes. Heaven, was that shade of blue, so soothing and pure.

But she shook her head. "How *do* you tell the difference between love and lust?" she asked instead.

He laughed in surprise. "You're asking the wrong man. My experiences with love are extremely limited."

Sandy smiled up at him. "Come on, McCade. I've known you for fifteen years, and you've been in love at *least* twenty different times—"

"It wasn't ever real," he told her. "I've really been in love just once."

"So there *are* differences. Tell me what they are."

He shook his head. "Kirk—"

"Please. You're the only person in the world I can talk to about this."

He was silent, just looking down at her as they danced.

"Did you know it was love before or after you slept with her?" Sandy asked.

McCade shook his head and rolled his eyes. "Sandy—"

"*McCade.*" She imitated him.

"Before," he told her. "I knew before."

"You're positive?"

"Very," McCade said.

"How can you be so sure?"

"Because I never made love to her."

McCade could see surprise in her eyes. "You're kidding."

"Can't we talk about something else?" he said a little desperately. "Have you seen Spike Lee's latest movie yet?"

"How could *you* be in love with someone and not—"

"Look, it takes two to tango, Kirk." McCade smiled grimly. "All right? Now, can we drop this?"

Sandy studied his handsome face. His arms felt so solid around her, and he was holding her close enough so that their thighs brushed as he moved. They fit together perfectly, just as he had said they would— Wait. He'd been talking about Sandy and *James*, not Sandy and himself.

She closed her eyes, imagining a world where Clint McCade saw her as a woman, not just a friend. He would hold her even closer, and she would melt against him, and . . . "I'm sorry, but I don't believe it. There's no woman on earth who would refuse *you*."

McCade just laughed.

FOUR

Sandy threw her keys onto the coffee table, and herself onto the couch.

"Wow, that was incredibly *not* fun," she said into the soft cushions. "James Vandenberg obviously finds me about as appealing as flat beer."

"Could be worse," McCade volunteered, shrugging out of his jacket and sitting down in the rocking chair across from her. "He could find you about as appealing as *warm* flat beer."

She lifted her head to look at him. "Cheer me up, why don't you, McCade?"

He unfastened his bow tie and began unbuttoning his shirt. "What do you know about body language?"

"Not much."

"Hmm."

Sandy sat up. "And just what is 'hmm' supposed to mean?"

"Whenever I saw you talking to James, you were giving him 'go away' signals with your body." McCade unbuttoned the cuffs of his shirt. "You crossed your arms and you stood with your legs tightly together. Your posture and your stance read 'don't touch' loud and clear."

"I wasn't doing it intentionally—"

McCade yanked his shirt free from his pants and shrugged it off. "That's the deal with body language. Most of the time it's done unconsciously. Somewhere down the line you've forgotten your female courting techniques."

Sandy shifted in her seat, crossing her arms. "This is all news to me. How could I have forgotten something that I was never told?"

"Defensive posture." McCade pointed to her crossed arms before he pulled off his boots. "You just told me with your body that you don't like what you're hearing, and you're not going to listen to me."

"And exactly which issue of *Playboy* did you read this in, McCade?" Sandy asked, her arms still firmly crossed.

"Look"—McCade sat next to her on the couch— "I'm going to hit you with some male courting techniques, and if you can honestly say that you still think it's a load of garbage after that, then I'll shut up, all right?"

Wearing only a sleeveless undershirt with his tuxedo pants, he looked like the McCade she knew in high school. He sat comfortably at one end of the couch, facing her, his right leg bent at the knee and angled across the cushion in front of him. He raked his fingers through his short hair, making it look perfectly tousled and very sexy.

Sandy lowered her gaze and shrugged. "Fire away."

"First of all, don't sit like that," he said. He pulled her so that she faced him, lifting her left arm up so that it lay along the back of the couch. He dropped her right hand into her lap. With their knees almost touching, he leaned, then inched forward slightly.

"Step one: Invade the woman's personal space. Step two: Direct eye contact." He smiled into her eyes.

Sandy smiled back. "This is silly—"

"I'm not finished," he interrupted. "Without saying a word, a man can let a woman know quite clearly that he's interested in her. Sexually interested."

McCade let his eyes drop, focusing for a moment on her lips, then traveling even lower, lingering on the low neckline of her dress. Sandy felt the urge to giggle, but by the time he'd slowly dragged his gaze back to her eyes, her mouth was dry and that urge was long gone.

"That's step number three," he told her. "And if by now the woman hasn't run away or threatened physical harm, a man might try step four—a nonsexual touching gesture, something harmless like a handshake . . ."

He lifted her hand, drawing her fingers into his.

". . . but he'd turn that handshake into a caress." He ran his thumb lightly over the back of her hand. "This is not just a friendly touch—the message has clear sexual overtones."

Sandy stared down at her hand as he continued that slight but oh-so-sensuous movement of his thumb. She looked up to find his eyes running down the length of her legs. He took his time before he met her gaze.

She could see heat in his eyes.

This was just a demonstration, she reminded herself. He was putting on a show, giving an example. Carefully, she slipped free from his grasp.

"If the touching doesn't work," he continued, his husky voice soft, "or if the situation doesn't allow for physical contact, there's always surrogate touching." He smiled, a quick flash of teeth. "I know, it sounds terrible, but it's not."

As Sandy watched, McCade used one finger to trace

the floral pattern on the fabric that covered the couch. He looked up at her and smiled slightly. "It sends out a signal that says, I'd really rather be touching you."

The small movement of his hand made the muscles in his shoulder and arm flex enticingly in the dim living-room light. He moistened his lips with the tip of his tongue and Sandy's mouth went dry.

"McCade," she started, but her voice sounded hoarse. She cleared her throat and crossed her arms again. "You could obviously write a how-to manual on picking up women. What I don't get is what male courting techniques have to do with me?"

"James was giving you signals this evening, and all you did was back away." He stood up. "I'm getting a beer—want one?"

Sandy nodded. "Thanks."

"One thing I didn't mention," he called from the kitchen.

She heard the refrigerator door open and then shut.

"Preening," he continued. "Both men and women do it if they're attracted to each other." She heard the hiss of the bottles being opened, the clatter of the tops as McCade tossed them into the garbage. "A man might adjust his tie, smooth down his hair—that's what James did. This is all done unconsciously, remember."

In the kitchen, McCade ran his hands under the cold water from the sink. She'd been sitting there, watching him, and it had taken all of his control not to sweep her into his arms and carry her into the bedroom.

Not that she would ever go willingly.

He closed his eyes, and in a sudden flash he could imagine Sandy, soft and willing, her body cradling his as she drew him back with her onto her bed—

McCade dried his hands on a paper towel, then used it to mop the perspiration from his forehead.

He went back into the living room and handed her one of the cold beers.

"So old James is sending you signals," he told her, getting back to the subject as he sat down on the couch again, "and what do you do? You cross your arms and freeze him out." He gave her a sidelong glance. "Same way you did to me just a few minutes ago."

He leaned back, putting his feet up on the coffee table as he tilted his head and nearly finished his entire beer. Sandy waited until he pulled the bottle away from his mouth before she punched him in the arm.

"I did *not* freeze you out," she said.

"Oh yes, you did."

"How *do* you know so much about body language?" she asked, her eyes narrowed slightly.

He shrugged. "I don't know, I read something about it once, and it really seemed to make sense, so I paid attention. I mean, I had already seen examples of different kinds of body language as I watched people. After I read that book, I knew how to interpret it." His smile turned sheepish. "For a while I *did* use it to pick up women. I could walk into a room, and within a few minutes I would know who was available and who wasn't. It worked every time."

"I'll bet it did," Sandy muttered.

"But we're getting off the subject. You need to relearn your female courting techniques."

"Which are . . . ?"

"Palming," McCade told her.

She started to laugh. "I'm almost afraid to ask."

He grinned and held out his hand, palm up. "It's a gesture of surrender. It's nonviolent, nonthreatening.

Studies of body language show that women in particular present the palms of their hands to the men that they're interested in. I think it's a passive-versus-aggressive thing, man being traditionally more aggressive, the woman being passive, you know, surrendering. A prize to be won."

"Ick." Sandy made a face.

"Yeah, I know." McCade had to laugh. "But ten to one says James Vandenberg doesn't know the slightest thing about body language, but he *will* unconsciously recognize any of these signals that you send him."

"What, so you're saying I should walk up to him and hold out the palms of my hands?" she asked.

"It's more subtle than that." He turned to face her. "Push your hair back from your face."

Sandy did.

"Oh, baby. You just flashed me your palm."

"I did not."

"Did too," he countered. "Instinctively, somewhere, probably at the very base of your brain where all your hormones bubble, your body recognizes that I'm a man."

"Hormones bubble?" Sandy snorted. "Very scientific."

"In addition to palming, all of the male courting techniques also work with women. You know, invading personal space, eye contact, surrogate touching . . . Oh, here's a woman thing. A leg thing."

He sprang up, pulling her legs out from where they were curled underneath her on the couch. He quickly slipped her shoes back onto her feet.

"McCade," she complained.

"Sit up, sit up," he said impatiently.

"All right, I am. Jeez."

"Now cross your legs."

The soft sound of expensive-nylon-clad legs rubbing together seemed to echo in the room. McCade felt himself start to sweat again. Sandy's skirt inched up, and she moved to push it back down.

McCade stopped her. "If you fix your skirt, then the message you send out is that you wanted to sit comfortably. If you let it ride up a little, you're courting."

"Courting what?" she asked, pushing her skirt down anyway. "Disaster? This skirt rides up much more, I'm going to be arrested."

"You know what I think?"

"I never know what you think, McCade."

"I think in order to be a successful businesswoman, you've had to alter your body language," he mused. "You purposely keep your eye contact and your movements to a minimum, because as a woman, you have to be sure you don't send out the wrong signals. Maybe it's harder to deal with James on a romantic level since he's also a business associate."

"Thank you, Dr. Freud," Sandy said. "What, no comment on my mother's influence on my life?"

"If you want James to know you're interested"—McCade ignored her, finishing off the last of his beer—"you've gotta tell him, and the easiest way to do that is with your body."

Sandy slowly drank her own beer. "You never told me the third thing," she said suddenly.

He frowned. "What third thing?"

"Your mother said there were three things men needed to learn in order to succeed. One was how to dance. Two was how to do research. What's three?"

"When it comes to making love," McCade said with

a smile, "and I quote, 'The size of a man's heart is more important than the size of his penis.'"

Sandy blushed. "She did *not* say that. McCade, you're so full of crap."

McCade's smile turned into a grin. "I swear, those are her exact words. I'm not even paraphrasing."

"There's no way your mom would *ever* have said the P-word. I refuse to believe that."

"She also gave me a box of condoms every year for my birthday—starting when I was twelve."

Sandy laughed. "No way!"

"She wanted me to get used to the idea of taking responsibility for birth control."

Sandy could remember Mrs. McCade, a quiet, worn-out woman with fading brown hair and a shy smile. "I can't believe it."

"Yeah, well, people are full of surprises," he told her. "What you see is not always what you get. And that's the *real* lesson she taught me."

McCade's mother had died halfway through his senior year in high school.

"I still miss her," Sandy said softly.

"Yeah," he said. "I do too."

"Boy." Sandy finally looked up from her plate. "I was starved. Did I have lunch today?"

"Not while I was looking." McCade leaned forward from the rocking chair to grab another slice of pizza.

She flopped back on the couch. "Now that I'm not hungry any longer, I'm exhausted. I may not live through five weeks of this. And tomorrow I've got to work camera number two myself. O'Reilly's grandfather just died, and he's got to fly to Montana for the funeral."

"What's on the schedule tomorrow?"

"Harcourt's speaking at the teachers'-union picnic." She closed her eyes. "And James is going to be there too. What am I going to wear?"

"You should wear what you've got on right now," he told her. "Shorts and a halter top. It's very sexy."

Surprised, Sandy opened her eyes and looked over at him. But he was busy, digging in the pizza box for the last slice of pie. She turned so that she was facing him, and propped her head up on her hand. "McCade."

"Hmm?" He still didn't look up.

"Will you do me a favor?"

He did look at her then, his eyes a flash of brilliant blue in his tanned face. He put his plate with the uneaten slice of pizza down on the coffee table next to his can of soda and stood up, wiping his hands on a napkin. "What, do you want a back rub?" He stood next to the couch. "Roll over."

Bemused, Sandy tilted her head up. He seemed so stern, standing there that way, looking down at her, un-smiling.

When she didn't answer immediately, he sat down next to her on the couch, nudging her over to make room. She turned obediently onto her stomach, resting her head on her folded arms. She felt the hard length of McCade's muscular thigh pressing against her as he brushed her hair aside. Then his strong fingers caressed her bare back.

She closed her eyes. His hands were gentle as he touched her, kneading the tension from her shoulders and neck. It was heavenly. His touch was tender, almost intimate, like that of a lover— Instantly, her perceptions heightened and she became extremely aware of

McCade's jean-clad leg against hers. What was it he'd said? Step one, invade the woman's personal space—

She opened her eyes and lifted her head to look back at him. But he met her gaze briefly, still not smiling, then looked down at his hands as he continued to massage her back. As she watched, his jaw muscle tightened, as if he were clenching his teeth.

Sandy put her head back down, resting her chin on the backs of her hands, convinced she was imagining things. Clint McCade was *not* using body language to give her any hidden messages. No way. If he was, he'd forgotten step number two—eye contact.

"Will you promise not to stop doing that if I make a confession?"

McCade hesitated slightly at her words. A confession? "Okay," he managed to say evenly, hiding the sudden acceleration of his pulse. "Confess away."

"A back rub wasn't the favor I was going to ask for."

Hah. So much for her confessing that she was madly in love with him. "It wasn't?"

"I was going to ask you . . ." As his hands moved up her neck she tilted her head to give him better access.

"What?"

"When we're in public, would you mind calling me Cassandra?"

His hands stopped moving and she looked up at him. "I know it sounds strange, but people around here think of me as Cassandra, and if they hear you call me Sandy, then they'll start calling me that, too, and—"

"Cassandra," McCade repeated.

"It's stupid, I know. But, see, I'm going to be thirty in a few years, and I want people to call me Cassandra, not Sandy. Sandy sounds like a cheerleader or Gidget's best friend or something. So young and, well . . . Do you know what I mean?"

He began rubbing her back again. "No, but if it's what you want, hell, I'll do it. Cassandra," he said, trying it out. "It *is* a pretty name. You're going to have to help me remember, though."

She nodded, closing her eyes again. "Thanks, Mc-Cade," she murmured sleepily. "You're a pal. . . ."

"Yeah," he said softly. "I know."

Her breathing grew slow and steady. He stood up tiredly and found a blanket to pull over Sandy. Cassandra, he corrected himself.

The name fit her. It fit her elegant looks, her powerful position as president of a thriving company, her place in the society of upper-class, country-club Phoenix. Cassandra Kirk. Not Sandy. Cassandra.

Damn, he thought. He wanted Sandy. Sandy was the sweet-faced little girl who followed his lead in and out of trouble, who needed him—his friendship, his advice, his help. Cassandra was a grown woman—sophisticated, elegant, and quietly in control. And after she snared James Vandenberg IV, Cassandra wouldn't need McCade any longer. There'd be no room in her life for him.

But right now she needed his help. And maybe . . .

Maybe this situation wasn't as hopeless as it seemed. Maybe McCade could use Sandy's infatuation with James Vandenberg to his advantage.

Yeah, she needed his help. So he'd give her help. Oh, yeah. Help, and a whole lot more.

FIVE

"Hi."

Startled, Sandy looked up from loading her camera into the back of the equipment van. James stood in the parking lot, smiling at her.

"Hi," she said, wishing as soon as the word was out of her mouth that she had said something amazingly clever instead.

"I didn't know you actually did camera work, too." James took off his expensive-looking sunglasses and glanced down at the portable camera she'd worn on her shoulder nearly the entire afternoon. It was on the floor of the van right now, and he motioned toward it. "It's a lot bigger than the camcorder I have at home."

Self-consciously, Sandy pushed escaped tendrils of her hair out of her face. She'd worn her hair back in a French braid, but after several hours of hard work capturing Simon Harcourt on videotape in the hot afternoon sun, her braid was ready to collapse—along with the rest of her. Her safari shorts were grubby and the neon-pink tank top she had on was covered with a fine layer of reddish Arizona dust.

James was smiling at her, and she made herself hold his gaze. Eye contact, she thought, hoping she didn't look as frightened as she felt. His smile was warm, though, and nice. But not as nice as McCade's . . .

James glanced back at the camera. "May I?" he asked. Sandy nodded, and he picked it up.

"Whoa." He grimaced. "I had no idea a camera like this would be so heavy. You carried this around all day?"

Sandy smiled at the irony of him admiring her for her strength. "Just the afternoon. One of my crew had a family emergency. I had to take his place."

"I'm impressed." He put the camera back down. "Remind me not to get you mad at me."

Was he flirting with her? Oh, brother, he was flirting with her! Flustered, she gave all of her attention to packing the camera into its carrying case. She locked the case down, attaching it firmly to the side of the van.

"You must be tired," James said.

"Nothing a shower and a cold soda won't cure." She moved to the edge of the van, about to jump down. But her foot caught on a wire, and she tripped.

Across the parking lot, McCade watched in alarm as Sandy launched headfirst out of the van. Her arms were outstretched, but he knew her hands would do little to protect her against the hard gravel of the driveway. He ran toward her futilely, well aware that there was no way he could reach her in time.

But James was there, and he caught her, and McCade skidded to a stop. His relief turned quickly to jealousy as the man held her tightly in his arms, and didn't release her. And didn't release her. And *still* didn't release her. McCade counted to ten before the lawyer stepped back. But even then, the man's hands lingered on her shoulders, then on her arms.

Wishing desperately that he could hear their conversation, McCade watched Sandy as she talked. She held her body tightly, stiffly, but as she spoke she gave James a beautiful smile and McCade's stomach hurt. True, she hadn't quite mastered the body-language thing, but there was no man alive who could resist a smile that sweet. God knows *he* couldn't.

As McCade continued to watch, her shoulders got tighter and she stuck her hands into the front pockets of her shorts. James's hand dropped from her arm, and she almost imperceptibly moved back, away from him. Her arms weren't crossed in front of her, but they might as well have been. Even from McCade's distance, he could see her tension, her discomfort, her shyness.

James handed her something, smiled, then walked away.

Sandy turned to look at McCade, and he quickly busied himself, loading equipment into the other van.

It didn't take too much longer to get the rest of the gear packed, and the vans moved out, heading back to the studio. McCade crossed the parking lot, heading toward Sandy, who slumped tiredly against her little car.

"Want me to drive?" he said into her ear.

She didn't even open her eyes, she simply held out the car keys. "Now, if only you could magically get me inside the car," she said, then gasped as he swung her up into his arms.

"McCade!" she protested as he carried her around to the passenger side of the car. He opened the door effortlessly, still holding her in his arms, and gently set her down in the seat.

"Not quite magic," he said, fastening the seat belt around her. "But it did the trick."

He crouched next to the car, one hand on the open door, the other on the back of her seat.

"You're spoiling me," Sandy said tiredly. "If you keep taking care of me like this, I'm going to go into terrible withdrawal when you leave."

"What if I don't leave?"

Sandy sat up, instantly awake. "What?"

But he had already shut the door. As he slid in behind the wheel she nearly pounced on him. "Clint, are you thinking of staying in Phoenix for a while?"

McCade shifted into reverse, adjusting the rearview mirror. Sandy called him Clint only when the subject was of the utmost importance to her. Since his mother had died, she was the only person who ever called him by his first name. In fact, through the years, he'd even discouraged his girlfriends from calling him anything but McCade. Clint was too vulnerable. Clint was a twelve-year-old little boy, alone and angry in a new school, outraged that his father had deserted him and his mother, forcing them to move to a tiny basement apartment in a bad part of town.

It was Sandy, who moved into that same run-down apartment building the following September, who started calling him McCade. She'd expected him to be some sort of tough-as-nails street kid, and so that's what he'd become. Her blatant hero worship left him no time to feel sorry for himself. She was a year younger, a skinny blonde waif, and he quickly learned to enjoy the role of her protector. An unnecessary role, McCade admitted to himself with a smile. He'd found *that* out after she'd attacked a ninth grader for making insinuations about McCade's paternity. She gave the boy, who was nearly twice her size, a bloody nose and a bruise on his shin that he'd no doubt remembered for a *long* time. After that, McCade and Sandy's friendship became more equal.

As he drove through the late-afternoon traffic he could feel her watching him as she asked again, "Are you going to make Phoenix a temporary home base?"

He glanced at her, one eyebrow raised. "Temporary? Don't you want me in town permanently?"

"You don't do permanent." Sandy pulled her sneakers off, wiggling her toes appreciatively in the coolness of the car's air-conditioning. "At least that's what you've been claiming for the past decade."

"Maybe I've changed my mind."

Something in his low, husky voice made Sandy look at him, *really* look at him. He looked away from the road for the briefest of instants to meet her gaze, but even in that short blink of time she could see something different in his eyes. It was more than sadness. It was a kind of desperation that she hadn't seen before. At least not before this visit.

She turned to face him, lightly resting her hand on his forearm. "Clint, I can't shake the feeling that you're having some sort of crisis," she said softly. "I wish you would tell me what's wrong so that I can help you."

McCade braked to a stop behind a long line of cars at a red light. He moved his arm so her hand slid down to his, and he gently locked their fingers together. "I'll be all right," he said, praying he wasn't lying.

"You know that I'd do anything for you. Just ask."

McCade smiled and lightly kissed the top of her

hand before he released it. "I saw your graceful exit from the equipment van."

"You're changing the subject."

"Very perceptive."

Sandy was silent. Since when did McCade keep secrets from her?

"Did you do it on purpose?" he asked.

Sandy stared at him blankly. "Huh?"

"When you fell out of the van, did you mean to?"

"Yeah, I intentionally planned to look like a fool." She snorted. "I've found that really turns guys on."

"It works for me."

McCade was grinning at her, and she found herself grinning back. "Well, gee, I'll keep that in mind."

Now why was it so easy to flirt with McCade? She would never dare say something so suggestive to James. Maybe it was because she knew McCade was safe. She knew he wouldn't take her seriously, the same way she'd never mistake his flirting for something real.

"What did Vandenberg give you?" McCade asked.

"You *were* watching me. I thought so." She narrowed her eyes. "How was my body language?"

"It needs work," he said bluntly.

"But I thought I was doing okay," she protested. "I mean, James had his hands all over me. In fact, for a minute there, I thought he was asking me out. He said there was a reception at Simon Harcourt's country club tonight, but then he gave me the directions and told me to bring a date." Sandy sighed.

"That's what he handed you? Directions to the club?"

She nodded. "Yeah."

"You know what I think happened?" he asked, and she shook her head, waiting for him to continue. "I think Vandenberg was intending to ask you to go to this reception with him, but then you started backing away, so he backed off too."

"Backing away?"

"Yeah." McCade pulled into the condo lot, zipping neatly into Sandy's slot in the carport. He turned off the car and dangled the keys toward her. "This time you froze him out by jamming your hands into your pockets and doing a quick two-step away from him. He interpreted that as an impending refusal. So, being a normal, red-blooded American male, he decided to skip the humiliation of a rejection. Can you blame him?"

"I froze him out?" Sandy took the keys and slumped dejectedly in her seat. "I'm a social reject. A body-language illiterate. It's hopeless, McCade."

"No, it's not." McCade extracted his long legs from the tiny car and went around to open the door on the other side.

Sandy looked away, but she wasn't quick enough to hide the fact that her eyes were brimming with unshed tears.

"Aw, hell, you're serious." He crouched next to her so their faces were on the same level. "Hey, Sandy, come on. You can learn body language, but it's just like anything else. In order to really learn it, you need to practice."

"Practice?" she echoed.

"Practice," he agreed. His hair was a jumble of waves, one lock falling rakishly across his forehead. The muscles in his arms tightened as he supported his weight, his solid biceps stretching the sleeves of his shirt. "Let's go inside, get showered up and changed, and hit that country-club reception."

"You hate going to that sort of thing."

"I'll live. You need to be in public to practice."

"Won't I also need someone to practice on?" she asked. "James isn't exactly willing."

"You don't need James," McCade said. "You've got me."

Sandy's heels clicked on the marble tile of the country-club lobby. She stopped at the entrance to the ballroom where the reception was being held.

There had to be at least two hundred people there, but the ballroom was so big, they seemed to be scattered about, standing in small groups, sitting at tables that dotted the edges of the dance floor, and dancing to music performed by a trio of musicians.

The men all wore tuxedos, and the women wore variations on the dresses they'd had on at Saturday night's fund-raiser at the Pointe. Sandy spotted the woman who had worn the outrageous peacock-feather dress. Tonight she was covered in shiny blue fringe that shook and shimmied when she moved.

Sandy's hand was resting lightly in the crook of McCade's elbow, and he tugged her gently into the reception. She caught sight of their reflection in a big framed mirror on the other side of the room, and nearly laughed out loud.

McCade looked like a million bucks. He filled out his designer tuxedo to perfection and his sun-streaked brown hair gleamed in the dim light. He wore it moussed up and back, off his forehead, thick and wavy and just begging for fingers to be run through it. His gorgeous lips curved up into a smile and then a full-fledged grin as he met her eyes in the mirror.

"Man, would you look at yourself," he whispered to her. "You look unreal."

She did. She looked like someone else, not Sandy Kirk. She wore the little black velvet slip dress that McCade had bought. Spaghetti-thin black straps crossed her smooth, tanned shoulders and the dress's neckline dipped down between her breasts, a reminder that she wasn't wearing a bra. But the woman whose reflection was looking back at Sandy from that big mirror didn't need a bra. That woman, with her long, thick jumble of blonde curls falling down her back, with the long, slender legs covered with sheer black hose, with her spike heels that made her taller than almost all of the women in the room and most of the men, *that* woman was self-confident, beautiful, and well-adjusted enough to know that velvet wasn't exactly see-through, and that even without a bra, she was perfectly, adequately covered. Besides, Sandy thought wryly, there was no bra on earth that could be worn with a dress that dipped as low in the back as this one.

McCade was right. She looked unreal. But the truth was that she and McCade looked exceptionally unreal together.

Familiarity, she decided. They were friends, relaxed and comfortable together, and it showed in their body language. Body language, she thought wryly. Yeah, right.

"Now that we're here," she said, "what do we do?"

"How about we have a drink? You want me to get you something from the bar?"

"No way am I letting go of you." Sandy tightened her grip on his arm. "You go to the bar, *I* go to the bar."

"The most beautiful woman in the room won't let go of my arm." McCade smiled at her. "I think I can live with that."

"Careful with the flattery, McCade," she said. "I might start believing you."

He looked down at her, his eyes searching her face. "Would that be so terrible?"

She looked away, unable to meet his gaze, afraid of . . . What? She wasn't afraid of McCade. She was afraid of herself. Afraid she was going to give herself away, afraid she wouldn't be able to keep her eyes from his mouth, his lips. And McCade, an expert on body language, would know without a doubt that she wanted him to kiss her. Oh, God, she was dying for him to kiss her. What on earth was wrong with her lately?

She studied the tips of his black cowboy boots. "How about that drink?"

With a sigh of frustration, McCade navigated his way to the bar, trying to decide whether to get himself a beer or a soda. Caffeine or alcohol. Which would cool him down the quickest? He decided on the beer. As long as he didn't have too many, he'd probably be better off. But God help him if he drank too much. He'd probably end up throwing himself at Sandy's feet, begging her to have mercy on him.

"Would you like a glass of wine?" He leaned toward her in the crush of people gathered around the long bar. Crowds usually bothered him, but he liked this one. It forced Sandy to stand close enough to him so that he could breathe in her delicious scent. Mercy, she smelled good. She never wore perfume, but the mixture of the shampoo and soap that she used, along with the unmistakable musky scent that belonged to Sandy alone, was better than any bottled aroma.

He felt his body respond to her closeness. Oh, man, he wanted her. Right here and now. He wanted to pull her into the empty coat-check room, lock the door behind them, and—

"Can I get you something?" the bartender asked.

"Beer," Sandy said. "Right, McCade? Bottled and imported. Make it two."

She smiled at the bartender as he poured two bottles of beer into tall, V-shaped glasses. She handed one to McCade and raised the other in a small toast. "Here's to body language."

Their glasses clinked, and they both took a long sip of the foaming beer.

"Speaking of body language . . . " McCade moved her away from the crowded bar. "I think you should pretend . . ."

He took another sip of his beer while Sandy waited for him to continue. "What?" she finally said.

"Pretend that you want me." He was serious. He smiled as she gazed up into his eyes, but this was no joke. She had never seen him so absolutely serious.

Sandy was silent as he pulled her farther away from the crowd. When they reached a small, deserted cluster of white wicker chairs and a glass-topped table, he stopped and gently took her beer from her hand, setting both of their drinks down.

"First thing you need to do is relax," McCade said, and she realized she had her arms tightly crossed in front of her. "Start at least by pretending that you like me."

"McCade, I don't have to pretend *that*."

"Good." His smile widened as he took both of her hands in his, tugging on them slightly. "Now pretend I'm an old friend who's come into town. Pretend I'm just here for tonight, and pretend that you've just realized that you're in love with me. Pretend that you've only got a few hours to let me know how you feel, and pretend that you're not the type to blurt out the truth." He dropped her hands and stepped back, away from her. "What are you going to do?"

"This is silly," Sandy said. "Why do I have to pretend all of those things?"

"Because if I told you to pretend I'm a stranger who caught your eye, we'd get into an hour-long discussion on the stupidity of picking up a person you know nothing about. Besides, you're going to come on differently to a man you know isn't a potential ax murderer, like James . . . or me."

Sandy nervously picked up her glass of beer and took a sip. "But I don't know James well enough to be sure he's not an ax murderer."

McCade laughed. "Now you're stalling."

She frowned into her beer, watching bubbles escape from the amber liquid. "But I'm . . ." She shook her head. "I'm lousy at pretending, and on top of that, I'm lousy at seduction. It's a wonder I'm not still a virgin. Do you think it's too late for me to become a nun?"

"Yes," McCade said firmly. "Much too late." He took a deep breath. "You don't need to know how to seduce a man. You just need to know how to . . . let yourself be seduced.

"Trust me," he added softly. "Do you trust me?"

She nodded, looking down into her beer again.

"Use your eyes. Remember what I told you about eye contact?"

Sandy nodded again.

As she looked up to meet his eyes he smiled ruefully. "I'm reading scared in your expression. Shyness too. You've got to be bolder. Let me know you're thinking about sex."

"But I'm not."

"You should be. Watch me, Sandy. Cassandra."

As Sandy watched, McCade's gaze turned fiery, burning hot. He let his eyes sweep down her body, taking his time as he looked her over, inch by inch. "Can you guess what I'm thinking?" He glanced back into her eyes and she blushed.

"Yeah," she said. "But—"

She didn't go on.

"But what?"

"I guess I'm a little more old-fashioned than you, McCade. I can't just flip a switch whenever I want to and feel . . . lust."

"I prefer to call it physical attraction," he told her. "And with me it's not a matter of flipping a switch. It's a matter of dropping defenses, of letting something show that I would normally keep hidden."

Sandy stared at him, trying to make sense of his words. "You don't really expect me to believe that you find me that attractive," she said flatly.

"Believe it or not, Kirk," he retorted, a hint of annoyance in his voice, "I do. I've always found you outrageously sexy."

Laughing disparagingly, she turned away. "Right."

McCade caught her arm, nearly knocking the glass of beer out of her hands. "Dammit, Sandy," he hissed. "When are you going to stop knocking yourself? I've never lied to you, why should I start now?"

"I'm sorry, I know you're not lying." Of course he was attracted to her as a friend. And as for the physical thing, well, it wasn't news to her that he liked anything female. She just hadn't realized he knew she was female.

Sandy gently pulled her arm from his grasp. She didn't want to fight. She was tired and hungry and she wanted to go home. But she knew McCade wasn't going to let her leave until she came through with this body-language stuff. She put her glass of beer down.

She didn't have to pretend she wanted McCade. All she'd have to pretend was that she was finally in that perfect world she'd dreamed about so many times. She looked up at him, and let all the passion and all the longing she'd ever felt for him show in her eyes.

She held his gaze as a series of emotions flitted across his face. She could see surprise, disbelief, amazement, and finally approval in his eyes. It was followed closely by a flare of what must have been reflective heat.

"That's the look," McCade breathed as she gave him a very obvious once-over.

When Sandy looked back into his eyes, she smiled self-consciously and held out both hands to him, palms up. "How'm I doing?" she asked.

"Not exactly subtle, but it'll do. Dance with me."

"What? Why?"

"It's the next logical step," he explained. "You just told me with your eyes that the game you want to play is one on one. Unless I'm crazy or brain-dead, I'm going to respond by trying to get you into my arms. That's what dancing's all about. It's an excuse for people to hold each other."

"I'm not a very good dancer."

"You do just fine." McCade smiled. "Besides, this isn't about dancing. It's about sex. Think of it as foreplay."

Sandy felt herself blush. "McCade, I'm exhausted—"

"Just one dance, then we'll go. I promise."

"I'm going to hold you to that," she told him as he led her onto the dance floor.

Sandy felt McCade's strong arms surround her and

wondered why she bothered to protest. Dancing with him was heaven. It was absolute paradise. She gazed into his eyes, and his arms tightened around her, pulling her against his muscular body. There was no space between them, no way they could get any closer—at least not with their clothes on.

Sandy could feel McCade's hand on the bare skin exposed by the deep V of the back of her dress. He slowly moved his hand down, touching her lightly and so sensuously.

"Yeah." His breath was warm as he spoke softly into her ear. "You remembered step four."

With a start, Sandy realized she was stroking the back of his neck, twining her fingers in his thick, soft hair. Without thinking, she *had* followed McCade's fourth step. She had taken a normal, polite dance hold and turned it into a caress. But she'd done it naturally, without being aware. Gee, maybe there was hope for her yet with this body-language thing.

"Cassandra." He said her name softly. "You know, there's not a single man in this room who isn't watching us dance."

She felt his hand move up her back, underneath her hair. His touch felt sinfully good. His fingers sent both chills and heat racing through her until she was nearly dizzy.

"They're all thinking, 'What a lucky guy.' " McCade smiled lazily. "And you know, they're right."

The song ended, but he didn't let her go.

"Vandenberg's watching us too." His eyes were glued to her mouth.

"Who?" Sandy said faintly.

"Vandenberg," he repeated. "James?"

James. "Oh."

"What do you say we really give him something to look at?" he murmured. It was as good an excuse as any, and right now he desperately needed an excuse. He couldn't bring himself to kiss her without one, and mercy, he wanted to kiss her. "Maybe this will give him the right idea," he added, even though the only idea he wanted to give James Vandenberg was that this woman in his arms belonged to McCade, heart, body, and soul.

Sandy nervously moistened her lips with the tip of her tongue, and it was all the invitation McCade needed.

He used his left hand to push her curls gently back from her face as he bent down and brushed her soft lips with his own. It was torture, sweet, delicious torture. One taste, one tiny, little, almost nonexistent kiss simply wasn't enough. He could feel his heart pounding, and he struggled to keep his breathing steady.

But when he looked into Sandy's eyes, he couldn't stop himself. "I don't know," he said, ignoring the fact that the band had started another slow song and people were dancing around them. "Do you think he noticed? We better do that again, just to make sure."

He kissed her again, longer this time, letting his mouth linger. It was still as sweet, though, still as gentle.

"Come on. I promised I'd take you home." Almost desperately, he led her off of the dance floor. If they stayed much longer, he wouldn't be able to keep from kissing her again, and if he kissed her again, he'd give himself away. He wasn't ready for that yet. It was too soon.

"Cassandra Kirk."

He looked up to see James Vandenberg and another man on a direct intercept path with them. He swore silently as he put a pleasant smile on his face.

"James. Hi." Instantly self-conscious, Sandy dropped

McCade's hand and started to cross her arms. She caught herself and stopped, nervously pushing her hair back, then standing with her hands loosely clasped in front of her.

"I'm glad you could make it," James said warmly. He glanced at McCade. "Clint McCade, right?"

"Good memory." McCade smiled as they shook hands.

"Politician in training," James explained with an easy smile. "Cassandra, do you know Aaron Fields? He's with Channel Five News. He's agreed to supply us with additional footage of Simon Harcourt from their video archives."

As McCade watched Sandy all uncertainty seemed to drop from her and she became the president of Video Enterprises. She stood slightly taller, and was instantly confident, cool, and reserved. "Mr. Fields and I are acquainted, yes." She fixed Fields with a rather icy smile. She didn't offer him her hand, and McCade realized that she did not like this man.

Impressed, he studied Aaron Fields. Out of all the billions and billions of people in the world, there were just a very small handful that Sandy actively disliked. And because she was full of second chances and forgiveness for bad behavior, it was not easy to fall into that tiny subset of humanity. But somehow Aaron Fields had managed to do so.

He wasn't short, not exactly, but with Sandy in her heels, he was a good four inches shorter than she. The man looked to be in his early thirties, and his widening girth put a definite strain on the seams of his tuxedo. He was obviously falling prey to a changing metabolism. His hair was blond, and his face nearly florid from a recent sunburn. Despite the red glow, he was still handsome, but unless he started to detour around the cheeseburger stand and take a few more trips to the salad bar instead, he was going to lose his good looks. His face was starting to get fleshy, making his small, gray eyes seem even smaller. He was a former prom king, McCade decided, maybe even a former high-school football star.

There was a story here, and knowing Sandy, it was bound to be a good one.

Unaware of the undercurrent of animosity, James was talking about setting up a meeting where Fields and Sandy could sort through the vast footage that the television station had taken of Simon Harcourt over the course of the years.

"Call my secretary," Fields said. "Although, my schedule's heavy for the next few weeks. Of course, we could always do it in the evening."

"We should have an intern catalog the videotapes first." Sandy was obviously not thrilled with the thought of spending an evening with Fields. "That will take a few weeks and—"

"It's already cataloged," Fields said with a smug smile.

Sandy hesitated, and McCade understood instantly. She didn't want to be alone with this man. "I'll have my secretary call yours," she told Fields coolly. "Maybe there's some time during the day you can fit me in."

"James, you'll want to review this footage." McCade spoke up. "Why don't you try to be there too?"

Sandy glanced at McCade, uncertain whether he was trying to throw her together with James, or if somehow he had figured out what a sleaze bucket Aaron Fields was. He smiled calmly back at her, and her heart sank. McCade *had* to be playing matchmaker. How could he know about Fields? She hadn't known the kind of man Fields was when she first met him.

Of course McCade was trying to get James to spend time with her. That was the goal here. She felt a little foolish for hoping that those kisses had actually meant something. Had she really thought McCade had kissed her for any reason other than catching James's attention?

"Actually, evenings are better for me," James was saying. He looked at Sandy. "But I can try to rearrange my schedule if days are better for you."

Sandy shook her head. "You're the client. You should pick the time most convenient for you."

James glanced at Fields. "Aaron's doing us a great favor. Let's conform to his schedule."

"How about early next week?" Fields said. "Say, seven-thirty? And I happen to disagree with Cassandra. Viewing these tapes is going to be tedious. You might want to wait till we've had the opportunity to weed out the unnecessary garbage and—"

"I think he should be there," Sandy interrupted.

"It's a waste of his time," Fields countered.

She turned to Vandenberg. "James, may I have this dance?"

It was a non sequitur, but James didn't do more than blink in surprise. He glanced at McCade, who shrugged slightly. "Excuse us," James said to Fields, then followed Sandy onto the dance floor.

McCade couldn't watch. He didn't want to watch. But he had to watch. He couldn't take his eyes off of them.

"You know her well?" Fields asked.

McCade gave a noncommittal smile, watching James take Sandy into his arms. Damn, they looked good together. Sandy was elegantly blonde and James was darkly handsome. McCade's stomach hurt.

"She's gorgeous," Fields commented. "Got a body of a dumb blonde but the brain of a computer. Terrible combination. Women are like children, better seen but not heard, especially when all they can say is no, know what I mean? If Vandenberg needs me, tell him I'm at the bar."

McCade tried not to laugh. He could picture Aaron Fields expressing similar sentiments to Sandy—who would no doubt cut him down into little tiny pieces, wham, wham, wham, like the chef in one of those Japanese steakhouses. But McCade's smile disappeared as he looked back at James and Sandy.

James held her too close, and she had her head tilted back as she spoke to him earnestly. McCade had to turn away.

"And after the last time Fields was so . . . rude, I swore I'd never do business with him again," Sandy was telling James. "He's a creep. But obviously, he's got something you need, so—"

"We can approach the other network affiliates," he suggested. His chiseled features were rendered somehow more handsome by the sternness of his expression.

"But Five's the best." Sandy shook her head. "They've won the award for best local news seven years in a row. We have a better shot at finding good footage with Channel Five."

"I don't want to put you in an awkward position." James's face was serious, concerned. His brown eyes were so dark, in this light it was nearly impossible to discern the pupil from the iris. The effect was disarming.

"If you're going to attend this meeting, I'll be fine. It's when I'm alone with Fields that he acts like a jerk."

"I'll be there," James said quickly, his arms tightening slightly around her. His body was firm and muscular, but somehow not as powerful as McCade's. "You can count on me."

Sandy grinned. "I'll wear my steel-toed boots, and pack a can of Mace and a derringer in my handbag, just in case."

"Steel-toed boots?" he asked, eyebrows raised.

"You bet."

"Ouch."

"You bet."

There was a sparkle of amusement in James's dark eyes as he smiled at her. He was holding her the way McCade had, with his hand against her bare back. Inwardly, she frowned. James was holding her the same way, yet something was different.

"How long have you been seeing Clint McCade?"

She glanced up at him. "I'm not."

He looked confused, and she tried again. "Clint and I are just friends."

James nodded slowly. "Does *he* know that?"

She laughed. "Of course."

He nodded again, obviously not convinced.

"I have to admit," James broke the silence that they'd slipped into, "I was surprised when you asked me to dance. At the time it seemed a little inappropriate."

"Sorry," she said with a laugh. "I suppose I should have waited and told you about my problem with Fields over the phone tomorrow. It's just that dancing seemed like a good way to have a private meeting."

His hand moved down her back, his fingers trailing lightly along her smooth skin. "This is the best private meeting I've ever been to. Any chance we can schedule another?"

Sandy stared up at him. James Vandenberg wanted to see her again. He was touching her, caressing her much the way McCade had. So why the heck wasn't she melting on the floor in a puddle of desire?

The song ended, and she gently pulled free from his arms.

"How about dinner?" James asked.

"Call me," she said as he led her back to McCade.

"I will," he answered. "Definitely."

He smiled warmly into her eyes, nodded politely to McCade, and walked away.

McCade was silent as the valet went to get the car, thinking about the way James had held Sandy when they'd danced.

Now what? He couldn't just sit and watch while Vandenberg waltzed away with her. Except James Vandenberg was what Sandy had always wanted in a man. McCade was . . . just McCade.

Sandy shivered in the cool night air, and he realized she had no jacket. Without thinking, he put his arms around her, and she burrowed against his chest, slipping her arms around his waist, underneath his tuxedo jacket.

Sandy's Geo appeared from the darkness of the parking lot, standing out among all of the Cadillacs and Town Cars.

McCade shrugged out of his jacket and draped it around her shoulders. With his hand on the door handle, about to open the passenger's-side door, he saw James Vandenberg talking to one of the young parking attendants.

He knew from the way that Vandenberg was glancing in their direction that the man had noticed Sandy quite sufficiently already. There was no doubt in McCade's mind that this guy was going to be dreaming about her tonight.

And that thought made him crazy.

Instead of opening the door for her, he nearly yanked Sandy into his arms. He caught a flash of surprise in her eyes before his mouth found hers. And then, Lord have mercy, he was kissing her again.

But this was nothing like the kisses he'd given her on the dance floor. This time he kissed her fiercely, his tongue pushing past her lips to explore her mouth. Her tongue met his, and the world exploded in a blistering wave of heat and passion. He pulled her closer, even closer, his fingers lost in the thick swirl of her long, golden hair. Her slender body felt firm and tight against him. He heard himself groan, a low sound of want and need that astonished him with its intensity. Dazed and breathing hard, he pulled back.

There was shock in Sandy's eyes. "McCade, what . . ."

If she had called him Clint, he might've told her that he loved her. "Vandenberg's watching," he said instead, his voice raspy and harsh. He opened the car door and helped her inside, closing the door tightly behind her.

As McCade walked around the car he looked toward James. The dark-haired man *was* watching, and McCade met his gaze without smiling, giving him a look meant to warn him off. Except James Vandenberg didn't seem the type to quiver with fear from a dark look.

The valet had left the engine running, and McCade carefully pulled his legs into the tiny car. He could feel

Sandy watching him, her eyes still wide. He drove away from the curb without looking at her.

Sandy sat in silence, remembering the feeling of that intensely powerful kiss. God, how she'd longed for McCade to kiss her that way. And even though she'd imagined what it would be like so many different times, her fantasies hadn't even come close. It had totally blown her away. Her knees still felt weak, and adrenaline still surged through her system. She still felt flashes of fire and ice and—

This was what had been missing when she'd danced with James. It was this tingle, this thrill that had been absent. James's touch hadn't sent shivers up and down her spine. She hadn't felt any dizzying waves of heat and cold when he smiled into her eyes. Her insides hadn't turned to molten lava, her heart didn't beat harder—

The way it had when McCade touched her.

She was in trouble here. Deep trouble.

She wasn't in love with James. She was in love with Clint McCade.

SIX

As McCade drove, the silence in the car seemed to get thicker and longer. Sandy was staring out the front windshield. Her eyes were unfocused and her expression was somber. One glance in her direction told him she was deep in thought.

He shouldn't have kissed her like that.

No doubt she'd realized he was in love with her, and was trying to figure out how to let him down as gently as possible.

Maybe he should apologize. No, he was damned if he was going to apologize for doing something that he desperately wanted to do again—something he fully intended to do again the next time he got the chance. Except there probably wasn't going to be another chance. Unless he apologized . . .

"Sandy." McCade cleared his throat. With his eyes firmly on the road, he could feel the steadiness of her gaze as she turned to look at him. "Did I . . ." he said, then started again. "I guess I went a little overboard back there."

"It was, um, very realistic."

"I'm sorry," McCade said, then mentally kicked himself for lying. He *wasn't* sorry, not one little bit.

"McCade," Sandy started, and he braced himself. Here it comes, he thought, the "I just wanna be friends" speech. "Can we stop and get a pizza? I'm starving."

Her words didn't make any sense at first, they were so different from the words he'd been expecting. She wanted a pizza. She was hungry, not angry at him. He'd apologized and she was obviously giving the matter no more thought.

McCade didn't know whether to feel relieved or disappointed.

Chicken, Sandy thought, looking at her reflection in the bathroom mirror as she brushed her teeth.

McCade was out in the living room, lying on the couch, watching Dave Letterman on TV. He'd changed out of his tuxedo and now wore just a very brief pair of gray running shorts.

Even though he'd apologized for kissing her, there was still some kind of electricity—a new, extremely sexual awareness—that filled the air every time their eyes met.

But it was nothing, Sandy tried to tell herself as she washed the makeup off her face and put on some moisturizing lotion. McCade wasn't going to risk their friendship by having a fling with her. And that was all she could hope for from him—a brief affair, a fling. He didn't do love and marriage. He'd told her that himself more times than she could count.

Sandy sighed. She didn't want to have an affair with McCade, she tried to tell herself. She wanted a long, lasting relationship. And if the only way she could have long and lasting was if they stayed friends, then, by God, they'd stay friends. *Only* friends.

So why was she wearing nothing but a nearly nonexistent pair of black silk-and-lace panties underneath her bathrobe? Why did she have the urge to go into the living room, turn off the television, and let her robe drop to the floor? Why was she considering throwing herself at McCade, regardless of the consequences?

Sandy closed her eyes, remembering the way McCade had kissed her. God, she wanted more.

Would a night with McCade be worth the price? But life without McCade would be unbearable. If they made love, he would probably leave and never come back.

But, Lord, she wanted him. And she loved him.

She opened the bathroom door and slowly walked to the living room.

McCade looked up and pressed the mute button on the television's remote control. "You going to bed?"

"Yeah," she said, turning away. She couldn't do it. She couldn't try to seduce him. " 'Night, McCade."

"Good night, Kirk." His soft voice followed her down the hall to her bedroom.

She *was* chicken. But it wasn't the potential loss of their friendship that she was afraid of. No, she was afraid if she made a pass at McCade, he'd turn her down.

McCade was in the bathroom when he heard the doorbell ring. He wrapped his towel around his waist and went out into the hall. Sandy's door was still tightly shut, and he'd heard no sound or movement from her at all this morning.

The doorbell rang again.

McCade crossed to the door and opened it.

James Vandenberg.

McCade was as surprised to see him as he was to see McCade.

"I'm sorry," Vandenberg said. "I guess I should have called first." It was clear he hadn't expected to find McCade there—especially wearing nothing but a towel.

"I guess you should have," McCade said. "Sandy's—*Cassandra's* still in bed." The implication being that he had at one time been there with her. If that's what James Vandenberg wanted to believe, well, McCade wasn't going to bother to correct him.

James was doing his best to remain expressionless, but his mouth was a little too tight. "When Cassandra told me you and she were merely friends, I told her I didn't think that was exactly what you had in mind."

"Smart man. But then again, you went to Harvard, right?"

"That's right," Vandenberg said. "And I suppose you're one of those reverse snobs. If it's high quality or upper class, you automatically despise it."

"I don't automatically do anything," McCade said evenly, leaning against the doorjamb. "If I did, we wouldn't be standing here talking right now. I'd be kicking your butt back into your car."

There was a glint in James's eyes as he looked at McCade. "Is that some kind of threat?"

"You went to Harvard." McCade smiled dangerously. "Surely you can come up with some kind of intellectual interpretation."

James's eyes lingered on the dragon tattoo that decorated McCade's right shoulder. "You need danger and violence in your life, don't you, McCade?" he said. "On the outside you cleaned up really well. But the man on the inside's not so easy to change, is he?"

Straightening up, McCade laughed, but there was no humor in it and his eyes were cold. "You don't know a damned thing about me, Vandenberg, so just—"

"On the contrary," James interrupted. "Simon Harcourt's security team investigated every one of Cassandra Kirk's employees. I know *everything* there is to know about you, McCade. I know you didn't finish high school—"

"I passed the equivalency test—"

"Not until *after* you falsified high-school records to get into college—"

"Fine." McCade had the urge to shout, so he purposely lowered his voice. "I'm a criminal because I wanted a higher education—"

"You've been in jail two different times—"

"Once because I was part of a news team covering a demonstration that turned into a riot. The police didn't care who they rounded up and tossed into their vans."

"You were also arrested for stealing a police car."

"I *borrowed* it," McCade said coldly. "I had to get some footage I shot over to the studio fast for the evening news broadcast. I couldn't find a taxi. I had no choice."

"That prank got you a criminal record and ninety days in prison."

"It also got me an Emmy."

"Maybe, but you haven't won any awards for the way you treat women."

McCade's eyes narrowed. "Harcourt investigated my *personal* life too?"

"The longest relationship you've ever had was with Chardon Blakely," Vandenberg said. "You were with her for five months and seventeen days. The only reason *that* lasted so long was because you were out of the country for three of those months."

"I can't *believe*—"

"During the past ten years the longest you've ever lived in one place was the six months you spent filming a movie on location in Alaska."

"So I like to travel," McCade said. "So what?"

"So all *I* have to do is wait," he said. "Sooner or later you'll be out of Cassandra's life. I'm betting on sooner."

McCade fought to keep his temper in control. "Was there something you wanted?"

Vandenberg held up several videotapes. "I wanted to drop these off and it was more convenient to come by here rather than drive all the way out to Cassandra's office."

"That's the biggest load of crap I ever heard." McCade kept his voice overly pleasant.

To McCade's surprise, James Vandenberg laughed. "I know," he said. "Bad excuse. You're right. I really wanted to see Cassandra. But you already knew that." He held out the tapes. "Will you see that she gets these?"

"Yeah." McCade took the videotapes.

"Tell Cassandra to call me when she's ready to have that dinner date." At the black look in McCade's eyes, James laughed again. "Never mind. I'll tell her *that* myself."

McCade resisted the urge to slam the door in James Vandenberg's face. Instead he closed it gently, placing the tapes on the table in the front entry hall. Sandy's bedroom door was still closed, and he stood in the hallway, just staring at it for several long minutes.

Guilt.

It surrounded him, suffocating him. Why hadn't he told Vandenberg that he and Sandy really were just friends? Why hadn't he told him the truth?

Because McCade didn't want that truth. He wanted to be Sandy's lover, not just her friend. Damn, he wanted to be her husband. And now, in James Vandenberg's eyes at least, McCade was a whole hell of a lot closer to that goal.

But Sandy liked James. Sandy wanted James. McCade had promised to help her, and here he was doing the exact opposite.

He had a persistent suspicion that James had been right when he'd implied that McCade wasn't good enough for Sandy. Sure McCade looked the part of an upwardly mobile man—as long as he was wearing a shirt with sleeves long enough to hide his tattoo. But inside, he was still McCade. Money hadn't changed him, not for the worse, but also not for the better.

McCade slowly dressed for work in a new pair of dark green pleated pants and an off-white polo shirt—some of the clothes Sandy had picked out for him when they'd shopped for the tuxedo. He barely recognized himself when he looked in the bathroom mirror. Besides the tuxedo, it had been literally years since he'd worn anything other than jeans and T-shirts. The fanciest he'd ever gotten, if you could call it fancy, was the pair of leather pants he wore when he rode his Harley in the cold or at night.

But here he was, looking like an upper-middle-class clone. People did some crazy things because of love, and temporarily changing his wardrobe was well within the realm of sanity.

He sighed. Sandy was going to be mad when she found out that James had come over and found him in her condo. She was going to be *really* mad when she found out he had said and done nothing to correct James's obviously incorrect impression of what he was doing there.

She was going to be really mad when she found out, and she *was* going to find out, because McCade was going to tell her.

Or die from the guilt.

At seven-forty, McCade finished breakfast but Sandy still hadn't awakened. Hadn't she said something about an early-morning meeting? If she didn't get up soon, she'd be late.

He went to her door and knocked lightly. No sound. He knocked harder, then listened again.

Nothing.

The door was unlocked, and he opened it slowly. Her room was dark, the shades blocking most of the morning sunshine. As his eyes adjusted to the dimness McCade crossed to the bed.

Sandy lay on her stomach amid a rumpled tangle of sheets, fast asleep.

"Sandy, wake up," he said. But she was dead to the world.

McCade leaned over her, touching her lightly on the shoulder. "Yo, Sandy," he said, louder this time, and her eyes opened. "I don't think your alarm went off."

She lifted her head, looking toward the clock radio on her bedside table. "Oh, shoot," she said as she saw what time it was. "Oh, no! I have an eight o'clock meeting!" She clutched the sheet to her chest, pulling it with her off the bed as she ran toward the bathroom.

"McCade!" she shouted over the sound of the

shower. "I'm *so* late. Pick me out something to wear, will you?"

McCade opened her closet and stared at the rack of clothing hanging there. Something to wear. A pretty blue-flowered sundress that he'd ordered for her from a catalog was hanging among all of her other clothes. It had arrived in yesterday's mail, and had been waiting on Sandy's doorstep last night when they got home.

The sleeveless dress would make her look like an angel.

McCade reached for a staid, almost mannishly cut navy-blue skirt and jacket. There was no point in Sandy hanging around looking like an angel. Not when she was planning to take the latest footage they'd shot over to Harcourt's—and Vandenberg's—office later that day.

He put the clothes on her bed just as she rushed back into the bedroom. Water dripped from her hair, and she had a towel wrapped around her.

"McCade, it's going to be one hundred and fifteen degrees out there this afternoon," she complained as she caught sight of the outfit he'd picked. "You can't be serious. I'm *not* wearing long sleeves." She pulled the new dress from the closet. "Besides, I want to wear something pretty today."

Sandy pushed him out of the room.

"Why?" he asked.

Why? She was about to close the door, but stopped, looking up into his eyes. Because she wanted McCade to notice her. She looked down at the water that was dotting the floor from her dripping hair. "Because I think James is going to ask me out to dinner today."

"I've got to tell you something," McCade said.

"It's got to wait." Sandy closed the door and quickly dressed. When she opened the door, McCade was still standing there. He followed her to the door of the bath-room and watched as she stood at the sink, quickly put-ting on makeup.

"Look, Kirk, I've really got to tell you this," he said. "You're not going to like it, but . . ."

She glanced up at him in the bathroom mirror. "What didya break, McCade? My favorite coffee mug?"

"I wish."

"My grandmother's teapot?"

"No—"

"Not the mirror in the hallway." She stretched her lips to put on lipstick, then smacked them together, looking at herself critically. "I'm not sure I can deal with seven years' bad luck—"

"I didn't break anything. I did something," McCade said as she rushed past him. He followed her into the kitchen. "Actually, it's something that I *didn't* do."

Sandy grabbed an apple from the refrigerator and washed it in the kitchen sink. Holding it with her teeth by taking a bite, she tucked her briefcase under her arm and headed for the front door. She unlocked the safety chain and the dead bolt, then spotted the videotapes on the hall table. Picking them up, she took the apple out of her mouth and turned to McCade. "What's this?"

"Yeah, that's what I'm trying to tell you." He smiled ruefully. "Um . . . Vandenberg came by early this morning and dropped those tapes off. You were still asleep."

She took a thoughtful bite of the apple, staring down at the tapes in her other hand. Nodding, she balanced her briefcase on the table, and slipped them carefully inside, and looked up at McCade. "James Vandenberg," she repeated. "Came by. *This* morning."

It was McCade's turn to nod. "Yup."

Sandy fought the urge to giggle. This was about as bad as it could get. So why did she have the urge to laugh? "You answered the door."

It wasn't a question, but McCade answered anyway. "Yup."

"Before or after you took a shower?"

McCade studied the worn-out toe of his boot. "Um. After. But not by much."

"I suppose you were wearing my pink bathrobe."

He shook his head. "Nope. Just a towel."

Sandy could picture it, like a scene from a romantic comedy. McCade, draped in a towel, his hair wet and his muscles gleaming . . . "I suppose James assumed . . . ?" She let her voice trail off delicately.

"Yup."

"Oh, *perfect*, McCade." She leaned her head against the door. "I told him last night there was nothing between us."

"Yeah, he mentioned that, and, well, now he thinks you finally succumbed to my charms."

Sandy closed her eyes. If only she had . . .

"I'm sorry," McCade said. "I should have straightened Vandenberg out as soon as I opened the door."

"He probably wouldn't have believed you. Not many people would believe a man like you could spend the night in a woman's house and end up sleeping on the couch." She took a deep breath, letting it out in a long sigh. "Oh, well. I suppose it's fate. I suppose James and I aren't truly meant to be together."

She looked up to find him watching her intently, a strange expression on his face. It didn't seem fair. She'd lost her chance with James Vandenberg—not that she really wanted him—because he thought she was involved with McCade—who she really *did* want.

Why couldn't life be easy? Why couldn't McCade just realize how perfect the two of them would be together? Why couldn't he come to his senses and pull her into his arms and tell her that he was madly in love with her?

Because he *wasn't* madly in love with her, that was why he couldn't. He wasn't, and he never would be.

McCade watched Sandy's eyes fill with tears, and his chest felt tight. Damn, she was really upset about this. She really did like this Vandenberg guy. "Look," he found himself saying. "It's not that bad. All we have to do is . . . break up."

Sandy looked at him as if he were crazy. "What?"

"Look," he said again. "Vandenberg really likes you, right? He made that more than clear this morning. All you have to do is pretend that you and I are an item for a few weeks, until this project is over. Then we stage a fight and break up."

As McCade spoke, the idea began to appeal to him. He would have the chance to play Sandy's lover for several weeks. It was a role he could assume with absolute sincerity, and who knows? Maybe, with a little time, Sandy would want him to play it permanently, and much more realistically.

"We can set this up so that I'm the bad guy," he said. "You know, I'll dump you. It'll look as if I led you on and—"

"We pretend we're an item?" Sandy asked, trying to get it straight. "How much of an item? I mean, what exactly does that mean?"

McCade kept his face expressionless. "It means we keep up this charade by pretending that we're lovers."

Sandy glanced away, frowning slightly. How *did* lovers act? It had been so long since she'd been in a relationship. Did people still hold hands, or walk with their arms around each other? Did they kiss each other hello and good-bye?

She felt a rush of heat to her face as she considered the ramifications of having McCade kiss her regularly over the course of the next weeks. After a few days she'd probably become totally incoherent. After a week she'd probably throw herself at him. No, this definitely wasn't a good idea at all.

"This isn't going to work." She went out the door.

McCade followed, several steps behind. He smiled. This was going to work perfectly.

SEVEN

"Okay," Sandy said. "We're all clear on the schedule for this weekend?" She glanced around the conference table where James Vandenberg sat surrounded by her technical crew.

Late Friday night, the video crew was heading up to the Grand Canyon. Simon Harcourt owned a small cabin just outside of the national park and he frequently hiked down into the canyon with his family. This weekend, Video Enterprises was planning to hike with him and get it all on tape. A hike into the Grand Canyon would provide perfect footage for the bio piece—Simon Harcourt at play in Arizona's own natural playground. It was all about the environment, about good health, family living, *and* the canyon itself would provide a pretty spectacular backdrop. "Now, if only we can get a guarantee we'll have good weather."

"This is Arizona," Frank said. "That's about as good a guarantee as you can get when you're talking weather."

McCade was sitting across the table from her, and she glanced up to find him watching her. Again. All during the meeting she'd been aware of his steady, heated gaze. He'd been playing the part of her lover for the past few days, and even though he didn't touch her at work, he always watched her this way. Whenever their eyes met, he would smile. It was an outrageously sexy half smile. Combined with the look in his eyes, McCade almost succeeded in making even Sandy believe he was remembering every little touch, every single caress of a steamy, passionate night spent making love to her.

She pulled her eyes away from McCade and cleared her throat. "We should be able to get all the footage we need on Saturday and Sunday," she said to her technical crew. "But be ready to stay longer. Keep Monday and Tuesday open too. And Wednesday, while you're at it." She softened her words with a smile. "I don't want to hear any whining about prior engagements if we need to stay up north a few days longer. Got it?"

At the murmured agreement from her crew, Sandy stood up. "Let's hit the road, then." It was nine o'clock and time to get the equipment vans going. They had an eleven o'clock shoot with Harcourt at a local mall.

"Yo."

Sandy looked up from her computer as McCade poked his head and shoulders in through her office door.

"Yo yourself," she said with a smile. "You've got the day off. What are you doing here?"

He opened the door wider. He was wearing his trademark jeans and T-shirt and carrying a brown grocery bag. "I had this uncontrollable urge to see you." His husky voice was low, but Sandy knew her secretary was probably straining her ears to hear their conversation.

McCade leaned back into the outer office. "Hey, Laura, hold all of the boss's calls, will you? She's taking a lunch break. So, do not disturb. Got it?"

Sandy heard Laura's affirmative giggle as he closed the door behind him. He clicked the lock firmly—and loudly—into place, and she stood up. "McCade—"

"Time for lunch," he announced as he unloaded the contents of his bag on Sandy's desk.

"McCade, the entire office thinks we're having a passionate affair. Locking ourselves in my office in the middle of the day is *not* going to help matters any."

"We're just having lunch," he protested. He opened a container of chicken salad and helped himself to a forkful. "Mmm, this is great. You've gotta try this—"

"Right now half of my staff are devising some sort of office betting pool, probably having to do with the size of your smile when you leave." Sandy crossed her arms.

"You want to go to the movies tonight?" McCade asked, putting a large helping of three-bean salad onto a paper plate. He sat back, putting his feet up on the other guest chair.

"You're ignoring me, McCade," Sandy fumed. "I *hate* it when you ignore me."

He dropped his feet heavily back onto the floor and leaned over her desk. With one finger he pushed the intercom button. "Laura?"

"Yes?" The tinny speaker made Laura's voice sound higher and scratchier.

He pushed the button again. "Just wanted to let you know we're not having sex in here, okay?"

Sandy slapped her forehead with the palm of her hand.

McCade pushed the button again. "Okay?"

"Okay," Laura finally answered.

He looked up at Sandy. "Better?"

She was laughing despite herself. "My reputation is totally shot."

"Why?" asked McCade. He was serious. "You've made this company a really cool place to work, Sandy. It's very casual, very friendly, and very relaxed. You give your workers lots of slack, plenty of free rein. Are you so certain they're not going to do the same for you?"

He reached across her desk and began loading a plate with chicken salad, lettuce, and a generous helping of cut-up vegetables. He set the plate down in front of her chair, then pointed at it. "Sit."

Sandy sat down slowly.

"Besides, the pool has to do with *when* they think I'll pop the question, not whether or not we're getting it on." McCade shrugged. "I guess they assume that's a given."

"My staff thinks we're going to get *married?*"

"Frank offered me half of the take if I propose to you on the date he's picked," he said between mouthfuls of salad. "At ten bucks a head, it comes to about a hundred for him, a hundred for me. So two weeks from Saturday, I'm going to ask you to marry me, okay?"

"God, McCade." Sandy had been toying with her chicken salad, but now she put down the plastic fork and frowned at him. "You're about as romantic as a slug."

He grinned. "Just wanted to give you a warning."

"And what would you do if I said yes?" She glared at him. "Are you really willing to risk spending the rest of your life with me for a lousy hundred bucks?"

This was it, McCade thought. There would never be a better time to tell her that he was in love with her. But the words seemed to stick in his throat. He coughed and swallowed, then put his plate down carefully on the desk. "Look, Kirk—"

The phone rang, and Sandy picked it up. "Kirk," she identified herself. She listened for a few moments, then turned to her desk calendar, flipping through the pages. "No," she said. "No, I can't do it then." Another pause, and she flipped the pages back again. "Right *now?*" She narrowed her eyes, looked at her watch, glanced at her plate of food wistfully, then finally said, "Tell them I'll be right over."

She hung up the phone. "That was Aaron Fields's secretary. I was supposed to go over to Channel Five tonight to sort through their video archives for footage we might be able to use in Harcourt's bio. But James had to cancel, only he's over there *now*, and both he and Fields are free, so—"

"So once again, you don't get to eat lunch." McCade watched as she put on a fresh coat of lipstick.

"The alternative was to risk letting the meeting take place without James." She clicked her makeup mirror shut. "I'd skip lunch every day if it meant never having to be alone with Aaron Fields."

"You never told me why you don't like him."

"He asked me out to dinner about three years ago." Sandy's hand was on the doorknob. "I was stupid enough to say yes, and he took that as a global response for the rest of the evening. That, combined with his incredible charm and his winsome way with the English language—among other things—won him his seat of honor on my top-ten list of people to avoid."

McCade nodded. "Someday when you have more time," he said, "you can tell me what *really* happened."

How did he know there was more? Sandy knew he couldn't read her mind. If he could do that, he'd already know how she felt about him, and he'd have long since left town.

Frustration rose in her. How could he look at her like that, as if his feelings were hurt because she wasn't telling him the entire truth, when he himself refused to open up and tell her what was behind those flashes of pain she saw so often in his eyes?

"Sure," she said. "Someday. Like, right after you tell *me* why you left L.A. in such a rush."

"You better go." McCade glanced away from her. "Or you'll be late."

"Sooner or later you're going to have to tell me."

He looked up at her then, smiling as he met her gaze. His eyes were warm and so intense that Sandy caught her breath.

"Sooner or later I will," he agreed, then changed the subject. "Whaddaya say we catch a movie tonight? As long as your evening meeting has been canceled . . . ?"

Sandy hesitated.

"Your pick," he said, waving his words like bait in front of her.

She narrowed her eyes at him. "You promise you won't try to talk me into seeing something with lots of blood and guts and gunfire?"

"Cross my heart." McCade did just that. "Although I really want to see that new Bruce Willis movie. But I know how much you like Bruce Willis—"

"You didn't even take a breath!" Sandy said in mock outrage. "You crossed your heart, and you didn't even pause for an instant before you broke your promise!"

"You've been dying to see Bruce Willis. Don't deny it."

She opened the door. "Good-bye, McCade."

"You win," he called. "I won't say another word about any movie at all until after we buy the tickets."

She stuck her head back in the door. "Deal."

"And *then* we found this absolutely priceless footage of Simon Harcourt. You probably don't remember, but a few years ago there was a fire at a community center in south Phoenix," Sandy told McCade as they pulled into the parking lot of the movie theater. "It was was one of those places kids could go to hang out after school, you know, to stay off the streets. Anyway, after the fire, the contractors' estimates for the building repairs were so high, everyone thought that was the end of the center."

She unfastened her seat belt and got out of the car, continuing to talk as she locked and closed the door. "But Harcourt heard about it, and he had the building checked out. Structurally it was still sound—most of the damage had been done by smoke and water."

McCade and Sandy joined the line at the outside ticket window.

"So he got together with some of the kids and the community leaders, and—"

McCade slipped his arm around her waist. "And what?" he asked, pulling her close to him.

"And they organized a cleanup." Her voice sounded breathless as his hand accidentally slipped under the loose hem of her shirt. "McCade, what are you doing?"

Her skin was like satin. She felt soft and warm and so smooth beneath his fingers. He forced his hand down to her denim-clad hips. But that wasn't exactly safe territory either. Damn, he wanted to kiss her.

"We're supposed to be lovers, remember?" he said

instead, holding her firmly when she tried to pull away as the line moved forward.

"McCade . . ."

He encircled her waist with both of his arms, pulling her to face him. This was just another game to him, Sandy realized. And he *did* enjoy his games.

This particular game involved role playing. She'd always suspected McCade would have been as successful in front of the camera as behind it, and now she was more convinced than ever. He was acting as if he were in love with her, and that ardent look in his eyes could easily have been taken for the real thing—except she knew better.

"No one knows us here," she protested.

"Are you sure?" he countered. "You never know who might be around—someone from your office, or one of Harcourt's staff members. Phoenix isn't *that* big a city."

At her skeptical look, he laughed. "If you don't buy that, then at least consider this an opportunity to practice some body language," he said. "Come on, anyone who's watching would think that you don't like me very much."

The line moved again, and McCade released Sandy as they walked forward. She reached out and took his hand.

"This is a little more my style." She glanced at him out of the corner of her eyes. "Do you think it's enough to convince our audience—of which exactly zero are paying us a speck of attention, I might add—that I like you, McCade?"

"It's a start," he said with a smile, loosely linking their fingers together.

They reached the front of the line, and she had to let go of McCade as he took out his wallet. "Two tickets," he said to the woman in the ticket booth, "for . . ." He turned to Sandy. "What are we seeing?"

"You're *not* going to buy my ticket."

"We can argue about that later. Right now we're holding up the line. What are we seeing, Kirk?"

"What do you think we're seeing?" She couldn't believe that he didn't know. "The Bruce Willis movie, of course."

McCade nodded. "Of course." As he bought the tickets he glanced back at Sandy and grinned.

"You didn't *really* think I'd choose another movie, did you?" she asked as he pulled her toward the popcorn line. "How much do I owe you for the ticket?"

"Nothing. Zip. Zilch," he said. "This *is* a date, Sandy. Cassandra. And I'm buying you popcorn and a soda too. So don't try to talk me out of it."

Something in his eyes told her not to argue, and not even to tease. For some reason, paying for her tonight was important to him. It probably had to do with this role-playing game they were caught up in. Sandy knew that if she and McCade really were involved, he would insist on paying for everything.

It was clear that he was getting into his part, and like most things McCade did, he was probably going overboard. But just how far overboard was he going to go? Was he going to get so wrapped up in this game that he wasn't going to be able to stop playing even after they went home tonight?

She didn't want him to make love to her simply because he'd gotten swept up in a game. But how could she resist him?

McCade dropped his arm loosely around her shoulders as they waited for the teenage employees at the concession stand to fill two large paper cups with soda.

With his other hand, he pushed Sandy's hair back from her face. It was a tender gesture, gentle and loving, matching the soft look in his eyes. Her heart lurched, and she had to look away from him.

This was all just a fantasy. It looked like real life, it felt like real life, but it was nothing but dreams and wishes.

Unless . . .

Unless McCade got so caught up in all the make-believe that he actually convinced himself he really was in love with her. But then what? He'd stick around for a month or two, maybe three if she got lucky. Then he'd get restless and leave. However she looked at it, happily-ever-after wasn't in the cards. Not with McCade.

"So they organized a cleanup." McCade carried both of the sodas and the popcorn toward the theater.

Sandy stared at him blankly.

"You were telling me about that news footage of Simon Harcourt that you found," he reminded her.

"Oh. Yeah. The community center. Right. Well, Harcourt donated all of the supplies needed to fix the place up, and the people in the neighborhood did the work themselves. But—get this, this is the amazing part—Harcourt actually helped with the physical labor."

"No kidding," McCade said.

"Nope. We have footage of him hauling sheets of plywood up the stairs. He's in the background of an interview with the kids. Harcourt wasn't looking for publicity, he didn't say a single word in the entire clip. I'm not even sure the camera crews recognized him. He was just working, he looked like Joe Average, dressed in jeans and a T-shirt, you know? I wouldn't have known he was there if James hadn't spotted him. But we zoomed in and sure enough, it was Simon Harcourt. James was mega-thrilled. He nearly did cartwheels because this stuff is gonna be so good for Harcourt's image."

The theater was dim and cool and sparsely filled. McCade stopped next to an empty row of seats to the right of the center aisle. "This okay?" he asked.

"Considering that it's exactly where we always sit when we come here," she said dryly, "I'd say it's probably okay."

McCade entered first, but instead of sitting down in the seat next to the one on the aisle, he chose the seats all the way at the end of the row, by the wall.

Sandy stared as he put the sodas in the cup holders attached to the arms of the chairs. He walked back toward her, took her hand, and pulled her with him.

"Lovers sit near the wall, where it's darker," he explained.

A gentle push sent Sandy into her seat, and McCade sat down next to her, slipping his arm around her shoulders as if it were the most natural thing in the world.

The dim lights cast mysterious shadows across his lean face and long nose as he looked down at her. His eyes seemed to glitter, suddenly looking more green and brown than blue. Smile, Sandy silently begged him. But he didn't. He just stared at her.

Her stomach and her heart were involved in a competition for the most number of flip-flops per minute. She took a deep breath. "McCade—"

He tugged her toward him, reached with his right hand to pull her chin up, and stopped her words by covering her mouth with his own.

It was an exquisite kiss. Sandy couldn't remember ever having been kissed quite like this before. It was a slow, leisurely sort of kiss that started with McCade lightly running his tongue across her lips. It was a gentle kiss, but firm enough so that she knew he wasn't going to end it anytime in the immediate future. His tongue swept across her lips again, this time with more pressure, a silent request for passage inside.

Her lips parted before she had time to consider all of the ramifications of kissing McCade this way. And as McCade unhurriedly claimed her mouth, drinking her in, she stopped thinking. Spinning in a whirl of desire, she met each thrust of his tongue with equal passion, until there was no longer anything even remotely unhurried about this kiss. She heard him groan as he tried to pull her closer to him, but the arm of the chair got in the way.

He pulled back then, and Sandy slowly became aware that the lights had gone down and the movie previews had started. She stared at McCade in the flickering light from the screen, and caught her breath at the heat, the unhidden hunger in his eyes. For one split second she allowed herself to hope that he truly wanted her, that maybe he even loved her.

"Cassandra," he said, and her hopes burst like a soap bubble.

He knew exactly what he was doing. He was well in control. He would have called her Sandy, he never would have remembered to call her Cassandra if he wasn't. No, her imagination was running away with her. McCade didn't really want her, nor did he love her. This was all a game to him, and she couldn't forget that. She couldn't let herself get caught up in the fantasy, or she'd end up burned.

He leaned toward her, to kiss her again, but she made herself turn away, pulling free from his arms. She clasped her hands tightly in her lap so that he wouldn't see how badly they were shaking. Using all of her concentration, she stared up at the movie screen as if, instead of showing a trailer from some cliché-ridden comedy due out sometime in the fall, it held the answers to the secrets of the universe.

Puzzled, McCade backed away. What had just happened here? Mere seconds ago he had been kissing her, and mercy, that had been one hell of a kiss.

With his good looks and happy-go-lucky attitude, McCade was a stranger to female rejection. As the movie started he watched Sandy's profile with a growing sense of unease. What if she simply didn't want him? What if her feelings for him had been brotherly for so long, she couldn't see him any other way? What if he couldn't make her fall in love with him?

He studied her face in the dim light, aching with need, and scared to death that he was running out of time.

"I'm going to bed." Sandy stood in the doorway to the living room. McCade sat on the couch, reading a trade magazine.

He barely glanced up at her. "Okay."

"Good night."

He nodded, not taking his eyes from the magazine.

Sandy climbed into her bed, desperately tired, but unable to fall asleep. She alternated between staring at the strip of light shining into her room from underneath the door and staring at the clock.

A half hour passed. And then another. And another.

At one-fifteen the light went off, but she could still hear him moving around out in the hallway. She heard his quiet footsteps stop directly outside of her door, and she held her breath.

As she watched, the door quietly swung open.

She sat up. "McCade?"

He jumped and swore. "You damn near scared me to death!"

"*I* scared *you?* You're the one sneaking into my room, for God's sake!"

"I thought you were asleep," he said from the darkness. "I was looking for my keys."

"Your keys?" Sandy leaned over and clicked on the light on her bedside table.

"I changed my clothes in here yesterday and I think I put my keys somewhere. . . ."

McCade was wearing his motorcycle jacket and black leather pants that fit his long legs like a sexy second skin. But the night was warm—in the high seventies, at the least. If he wore leather, then wherever he was headed, he was planning to get there at high speed.

"Where are you going?" she asked, trying to sound casual.

"I need to go for a ride," he told her.

Need. Sandy's heart sank as she climbed out of bed to help him look for his keys. This was how McCade's restlessness, his urge to wander started. He'd go off on his bike in the middle of the night to roar along the highways, to feel the wind on his face and in his hair. At first that illusion of total freedom was enough to satisfy him, but eventually his midnight jaunts would get longer and longer. One day she'd wake up to find him packed and ready to leave. And then, as quickly as he had appeared, McCade would be gone.

They were on her dresser—a plain metal ring with four keys attached. "Found 'em."

McCade watched her cross to him with the keys. She was wearing one of those ridiculous little white cotton nightie things she liked to wear to bed. It was extremely sweet looking and demure. Except in this light the damn thing was nearly transparent. With her hair in an unruly jumble around her face and down her back, she looked so sexy it hurt.

"Can't you sleep?" he asked quietly.

He held his breath, waiting for her reply. Ask me to stay, he thought. If she would just ask him to stay and keep her company, he would tell her that he loved her and maybe—

"I've got a lot on my mind," she said. "I keep thinking about all the things that can go wrong this weekend up at the Grand Canyon."

Please ask me to stay. Their eyes met and something sparked, and Sandy quickly looked away.

She handed him the keys. "Be careful. I always worry when you ride at night."

It was clear that she wasn't going to ask him to stay. He swallowed his disappointment. "I don't have to go."

She just looked at him.

"If you want me to stay," he said quietly, "I will."

"No. You *need* to go, remember?" She shook her head. "Go for a ride, and get it out of your system, Clint. If you don't, you'll be strung way too tight for the weekend. And I need *you*—and your camera—to be at one hundred percent."

But he didn't need to go. Not anymore. He needed to stay. He needed to talk to her. He needed to make love to her. . . .

Sandy climbed back into her bed. "Good night, Mc-Cade."

❖———————❖

The phone rang. It was quarter to four in the morning, and the phone was ringing. Sandy groped for it in the darkness. "Hello?"

"Yo." It was McCade. "Sandy, baby, you still awake?"

It *was* McCade and he had clearly had too much to drink.

"I am now." She turned on the light. "Where are you?"

"Where the hell am I?" she heard him ask someone. She could hear bar sounds in the background—distorted country music and the unmistakable relentless ringing of a pinball machine. "The corner of Van Buren and Vine," he repeated for her benefit. "I'm in a real dive of a roadhouse called the Cactus Ranch. What the *hell* is a cactus ranch anyway?"

Sandy could hear a good-natured voice on the other end, but couldn't make out the words. Whatever the man had said, it made McCade laugh. "Shut up, Peter," she heard him say. "My *pal* Peter, the bartender, took my damn keys," he said to her. "He won't let me drive home and this dump is closing in less than an hour. I don't have enough money for a taxi, and Peter won't give me an advance on any of my credit cards. He says they don't take plastic here. I need you desperately, baby. Come and save me."

Baby? That was the second time he'd called her that. "Just let me throw on some clothes and—"

"But I like what you're wearing right now." McCade lowered his voice. "It's very sexy. Did you know that when you're backlit, I can see right through that nightgown?"

God, no, she didn't know that. She managed to keep

her voice steady as she pulled on a pair of jeans. "Van Buren and Vine. I'll be right over."

"Hey, Sandy?"

"What, McCade?"

"Don't tell Peter, but he's right. I'm a little drunk."

"A little," she agreed.

This part of Van Buren Street could not be mistaken for the garden spot of Phoenix. Near Sky Harbor Airport, it was an endless strip of cheap motels, neon-lit roadhouses, and fast-food restaurants. The street was deserted at this late hour, and Sandy wasn't sure whether that was cause for relief or worry.

The Cactus Ranch had a dirt parking lot with huge potholes. One dim spotlight lit the sagging front door of the ugly, squat building. A row of motorcycles stood out front. Other than the bikes, there was only one car in the lot.

She parked as close to the door as she could and got out of her car.

She'd intended to tuck her nightgown into her jeans and pull her denim jacket on—until McCade made his comment about being able to see through her nightie. After that, she felt obligated to change entirely, and now she wore a plain, blue cotton work shirt with her jeans. With any luck, she'd fit right in, no one would notice her, she could grab McCade and leave.

The door opened with a squeak, and she hesitated before stepping into a room filled with cigarette smoke and loud music.

There were about fifteen people in the entire bar, but most of them were big—even the women—and covered with leather and chains. So much for fitting in.

Sandy spotted McCade sitting at the bar, talking to the bartender—a friendly-looking man who seemed to be at least part Native American.

She ran the gauntlet of interested male and hostile female eyes and finally reached the bar.

"McCade."

He spun on the bar stool to face her and fell onto the floor. But he grinned up at her as if he didn't feel any pain. "Hey! Sandy! What the hell're you doing here?"

"You called me." She nudged him with her foot. "To come and take you home?"

"You must be Sandy. I'm Peter," the bartender said with a smile, holding out his hand. She shook it briefly. "You're actually as pretty as McCade said you were." He reached under the bar for McCade's keys and handed them to her. "We've all heard an awful lot about you tonight."

McCade was struggling to get to his feet. "*I* called you?" He frowned. "When did I call *you?*" He waved his frown away. "Hell, it doesn't matter. You're here now, baby, and that's what counts. Wanna dance?"

It was amazing. Even falling-down drunk, McCade still managed to be the most attractive man she'd ever seen. His hair was messy, he needed a shave, and he could barely stand, but his crooked smile was charming and his eyes were still an impossible shade of blue.

Very, very *hot* blue. He moved closer. *Step one—invade personal space.* . . . "Come on, baby, let's dance."

Sandy crossed her arms and took a step back. "McCade. I got out of my nice warm bed to come and bring you home. Assuming I ever make it back into bed, I have to go to work in less than three hours. So, no, I'm not going to dance."

"Mercy! Will you look at her body language," Mc-Cade said to Peter. "Is she mad at me, or what?"

"Go home," Peter said gently. "I'll keep your Harley safe. You can pick it up tomorrow, okay?"

McCade turned to Sandy. "Six women—" He looked back at Peter. "Six *different* women?"

"That's right."

"Six *different* women tried to get me to go home with them tonight," he said. "But I didn't want to go home with them."

Sandy stared up at him, unamused. "Why are you telling me this, McCade?" she asked. "So I can give you some kind of Boy Scout Merit Badge or something?"

"You know what I told them all?" McCade turned to Peter. "What the hell did I tell 'em, Peter?"

Peter smiled. "You told them that there was just one woman in the entire world you wanted to go home with. And that unless their name was Sandy Kirk, they should leave you alone."

She stared up at McCade's crooked grin. He couldn't have meant *go home with* in the same sense that other people meant that same phrase, or maybe . . .

Sandy shook her head. What was she doing analyzing what McCade had reportedly said? He was falling-down drunk, for crying out loud. He couldn't even remember calling her on the telephone, let alone what he'd said to the six women who'd tried to pick him up. *Six women . . .*

"Please, McCade, let's go." Sandy pushed at him gently.

"So long, Peter," McCade said over his shoulder.

"See you, McCade. Nice meeting you, Sandy." The bartender smiled serenely and went back to drying glasses.

The sky was getting lighter in the east as Sandy helped McCade into the front seat of her little car. She had to lift his legs to get his big cowboy boots inside the tiny space. God, there was so much of him. Finally, she got his seat belt fastened, untangled his fingers from her hair, closed the door, and climbed in behind the steering wheel.

They headed north, driving in silence for several miles before McCade suddenly turned to her. "Stop the car."

There was no other traffic, and she quickly pulled to the side of the road and into the parking lot of a strip mall. She put the car into neutral and yanked up the parking brake.

"What's wrong?" She turned toward him. "Do you feel sick?"

McCade kissed her.

He tasted like an odd mixture of whiskey, beer, cigarette smoke, and himself. God, she was actually starting to recognize the taste of his kisses. His mouth was warm, and his lips were soft, and she wanted to kiss him again, but she pushed him away. He was drunk. Somehow kissing him seemed like taking advantage. "McCade, stop."

He raked his hair back from his face with his fingers. "I don't want to stop. Kiss me, Cassandra. Please."

He watched her steadily, his eyes almost feverishly bright. Just how drunk was he? Sitting there like that, looking at her like that, he certainly didn't seem as drunk as he had when she'd nearly carried him across the parking lot of the Cactus Ranch.

But then he grinned, a silly, lopsided, out-of-control grin. "Please?" he said again. "Kiss me like you did in the movie theater—like you want me to take off all your clothes with my teeth."

Sandy laughed, a short, nervous burst of air. "I did not kiss you like that."

He laughed, too, his eyes dropping down to her mouth. "Oh, yeah. You did. Please, baby, kiss me that way again."

She looked away, embarrassed, but he pulled her chin up, turning her head so that she met his eyes.

"Please?"

He pulled her toward him, closer and closer and closer, and Sandy couldn't resist. As his mouth covered hers, she closed her eyes, clinging to him, letting him invade her senses, pulling his tongue deeply into her mouth. She heard McCade moan, felt his hands try to draw her even closer. But they were both seat-belted in, and he alternately cursed and laughed with frustration between kisses.

His hands were everywhere—in her hair, touching her face, her lips, running along her legs, up to her hips, to her waist, and then higher as he kissed her again and again. Sandy gasped as his hand found her breast, his thumb roughly teasing her sensitive nipple to life through her shirt and bra.

"Oh, Lord, I want you," McCade breathed. He yanked at her shirt, trying to pull it free from her jeans, fumbling with the buttons. "I need you, baby, please—"

He pulled too hard, and the buttons went flying around the car. But her shirt was open at last, revealing the delicate white lace of her bra and the paleness of her skin. He touched her, slipping his fingers underneath the lace, cupping the softness of her breast as he gazed into her eyes.

"I love you," he whispered. "Cassandra, I love you. Marry me."

He trailed kisses down her neck, down toward her

breasts as Sandy fought the waves of disappointment that threatened to drown her. McCade had lost his grasp of reality. She knew he was drunk, so why had she even let him kiss her in the first place? She felt tears welling in her eyes. This was her own stupid fault. He was caught up in his role as Sandy's lover, caught up in the game they were playing for James Vandenberg's benefit. Her tears started to escape, trailing down her cheeks, falling faster and faster. He didn't really love her, he was just pretending to. As for marriage, well, he was certainly confused about *that*. He wasn't supposed to ask her to marry him until a week from Saturday, or else he and Frank wouldn't win the office betting pool.

She pushed him away, holding her shirt together with both hands.

He stared at her, surprised and confused until he saw the tears streaming down her face. Then he was shocked.

"Oh, Lord have mercy, I made you cry," he said huskily. "God, Sandy, what did I do? Did I hurt you?"

He reached for her, but she flinched. "Don't touch me, McCade," she said sharply. "I don't want you to touch me!"

"Why not?"

Sandy put the car into gear and drove out of the parking lot with a squeal of her tires.

He put his hand on her knee. "Why not?" he asked again. "This is good. This is *really* good. . . ."

She pushed his hand away. God, it was hard enough to drive with one hand holding her shirt closed. "No," she said. "It's *not* good."

He put his hand back. "Come on—"

Sandy hit the brakes hard, and her car squealed to a stop. "No!" she said. "God help me, McCade, I said *no!*"

He had tears in his own eyes now. Poor, dumb, drunk McCade. He honestly didn't understand. The alcohol had sent him into a world that consisted only of the present, only of here and now. Right now he had no past and no future to worry about. Right now *now* was all that mattered, and for a short time McCade's now had seemed about to include a very passionate encounter with a female member of the human race. Namely Sandy—not that that particularly mattered to him in his present condition.

McCade was drunk, but Sandy wasn't. Sandy knew better, and more mattered to her than instant gratification. Yeah, sure, she wanted him, but she wanted him to want her too. She wanted him to want her as *Sandy*, not as some female who happened to be available. She wanted him to love her, not just get caught up in some game they were playing. And dammit, if they were going to make love, she damn well wanted him to remember it for the rest of his life.

He'd turned away, unable to stop his tears as the alcohol in his system took charge of his emotions.

Sandy wiped her own eyes on the sleeve of her shirt and put the car back in gear. "McCade."

He didn't look up, didn't acknowledge her.

"If you still—" She moistened her lips nervously, then started again. "If you still want to make love to me when you're sober," she told him quietly, "just let me know, okay?"

He looked at her then, wiping his eyes with the palms of his hands. "I'm pretty skunked, huh?"

"Uh-huh." She smiled ruefully. "And my bet is, you're not going to remember any of this tomorrow."

"Maybe," he said. "But there's one thing I won't ever forget. No matter how drunk I am."

Sandy pulled her car into the condominium parking lot. "What's that, McCade?"

She turned to look at him and he smiled at her, but it was an uncertain smile, making him seem young and vulnerable. "How much I love you."

She felt a fresh flood of tears well up in her eyes. "That's nice, McCade." She somehow kept her voice even.

"You believe me, don't you?" He sounded anxious.

"Sure," she lied. "Sure, McCade."

EIGHT

By the time McCade stumbled out of the shower, the painkiller he'd taken had started to kick in. Still, he moved gingerly, not quite sure his head was firmly attached to his neck.

As he dried himself off he tried to remember exactly what had happened last night. He remembered going out on his bike and riding hard and fast. He'd taken Camelback Road all the way out to Route 17. He'd gotten on the highway heading south, and went all the way down to the airport in record time. Then he'd cruised Van Buren, looking for a bar still open that late. He'd finally found one, he wasn't sure exactly where.

The gang inside had been doing shots of whiskey with beer chasers, he remembered. He recognized some of the men from the various cross-country road trips he'd taken on his Harley. After they'd teased him about his short hair, they all got down to some serious drinking and pool playing. Things grew a little hazy after that.

A *little* hazy? Try totally obscured. How the hell had he gotten back to the condo? He didn't have a clue.

He wrapped the towel around his waist and went out into the living room. Sandy had left a clean pile of underwear out on the coffee table.

Sandy?

He froze as he had a sudden flash of Sandy, sitting in the driver's seat of her car, her head thrown back, her lips moist and bruised looking from the force of his kisses, her beautiful eyes heavy-lidded with desire. And, mercy, her shirt was open, revealing her perfect breasts covered only by the white lace of her bra.

The room spun, and McCade sat down heavily on the couch.

What the *hell* had happened last night?

He squeezed his eyes shut and willed himself to remember. Nothing else came back. Dear God, he would remember if they had made love, wouldn't he?

McCade picked up the telephone. He got as far as dialing Sandy's office number, then hung up.

Damn, what was he supposed to say to her? Hey, how are ya, babe? Oh, by the way, did we get it on last night?

He took a deep breath, forcing himself to stop and think. If they *had* made love, he would have remembered it. For Pete's sake, he was desperately in love with this woman. Making love to her would have been an event of incredible significance. He *would* have remembered, no matter *how* drunk he'd been.

Besides, if they'd made love, he would have woken up in Sandy's bed, wouldn't he?

He picked up the phone again, this time to call a taxi. Then he finished getting dressed.

The ride to Sandy's office didn't take very long, but McCade put his head back anyway, closing his eyes and clearing his mind, hoping to fill in more of the blanks in his memory. He remembered there was a bartender, yeah, a really friendly guy by the name of . . . Peter? Smart guy, too, he thought, remembering that Peter had taken his keys away from him. Damn, if he had tried to ride his bike last night, he probably wouldn't be alive right now. Worse yet, some innocent bystander might not be alive either.

Why had he let himself get so utterly drunk? It had been years since he'd done something so foolish. But he needed . . . McCade opened his eyes. The things he needed lately were so different from the things he'd needed in the past. He'd gotten nothing from last night's ride on the highway. Instead of feeling a rush from the speed and the exhilaration of the road, he'd longed to be back at Sandy's. He wanted to be in her bed. And not just for the sex, although that sure as hell wouldn't have hurt. He wanted to hold her, to be with her, to love her. Man, he wanted to tell her she owned his heart.

For the first time in his life McCade wanted to stay. He wanted to stay with Sandy. Forever. He *needed* to stay. And the fact that she might not want him made him crazy. It scared the hell out of him.

So he drank last night to numb the fear. He got loaded and, the best he could figure it, woke her up and dragged her out of bed to give his sorry self a ride home.

Perfect.

They were scheduled to leave for the Grand Canyon this evening. He knew that Sandy's day was filled with important meetings and phone calls and all the work she had to get done before leaving town.

So what did he do? He made sure she got only a few hours' sleep. Yeah, he was a real prince.

The taxi pulled up in front of Video Enterprises, and

McCade paid the driver and got out, careful not to bump his still-throbbing head.

Inside the building, the receptionist smiled at him, and he slowly headed down the long corridor that led to Sandy's office. Her door was closed, and Laura sat outside at her desk like a secretarial bodyguard.

"She busy?" McCade asked.

Laura made a face. "Are you kidding?" she asked. "This is the first time I've been able to sit down all day. One of the cameras wasn't tied down properly in the van, and its lens cracked. We've all been going nuts, trying to find a replacement part that will be here by the time the equipment leaves for points north at three o'clock. So, yeah, she's busy. But she's alone, if that's what you really meant."

McCade motioned to the intercom. "Will you, um, let her know I'm here. Tell her that I'd like to see her—if she's got the time."

Laura looked at him strangely. "You two have a fight? You usually just walk right in."

"Just tell her, okay?" McCade's hands were shaking, an aftereffect of having had too much to drink, and he shoved them in his pockets. Damn, he felt sick. "Please?"

Laura pushed down the intercom button and neatly relayed the information to the inner office.

Sandy didn't bother to answer via the intercom. She simply opened her office door.

McCade caught his breath. She looked beautiful. She was wearing a loose-fitting white silk blouse, tucked into a baggy, pleated pair of khaki trousers that emphasized her slenderness. Her hair was swept up on top of her head in charming disarray. Strands of her curls were falling free around her face.

Yeah, she looked beautiful, but she also looked tired. And McCade was responsible for that.

She smiled at him, one eyebrow raised curiously. "Since when do you need an invitation to come into my office?" She stepped back so that he could come inside.

He turned to face her as she closed the door behind him. "I wasn't sure you'd want to see me."

Sandy turned to shut off the bright overhead lights and crossed to the window to close the blinds. The room became dim and soothing. "Better?" she asked, moving behind her desk.

McCade sat carefully in one of her guest chairs and took off his sunglasses. "Yeah. Thanks." He took a deep breath. "I want to apologize," he said, and her eyes flashed up and locked with his for one split second before she looked away again. Oh, Lord, he *did* have something to apologize for, didn't he? But what?

His face was pale underneath his tan and Sandy noticed that he moved gingerly. He looked like hell, and he probably felt ten times worse, yet he'd dragged himself out of bed to come down here to see her. How much of last night did he remember? Her own words echoed in her head: *If you still want to make love to me when you're sober, just let me know.*

He looked down at the sunglasses in his hand and played with the earpieces. Finally, he glanced back at her. "I want to apologize," he repeated, "but to tell you the truth, I don't remember exactly what it is I did that I need to apologize for."

He didn't remember. Thank God. Sandy straightened the papers on the top of her desk, lining up all the edges and corners. "If you don't remember, then how do you know you did something that needs an apology?"

"I was hoping you could answer that. Do I need to

apologize for anything besides waking you up in the middle of the night?"

She looked up at him again. "No." She smiled very slightly as she shook her head. "You don't."

But McCade swore softly under his breath. "Yes, I do. I remember. I made you cry, didn't I?"

Her silence was enough of an answer.

"I did." He swore again.

"It was late," Sandy said. "And I was tired—"

"What did I say?" he asked with dread. "Oh, damn, what did I *do?*"

"We had this exact same conversation last night. Just let it go, all right?"

"Sandy, I'm sorry," he said, leaning forward. "Whatever I did, it upset you, and I'm sorry."

"The apology's unnecessary but accepted, okay?" she said lightly, then opened her desk drawer and fished inside for her car keys. She held them out to him. "Take one of the guys and go pick up your bike. It's at a place called the Cactus Ranch down on the corner of Van Buren and Vine. I think Frank might be in the editing room. If not, Tom or Ed should be around here somewhere. One of them can drive my car back."

McCade took the keys from her. "Thanks."

"You think you're going to have steady hands by five o'clock?" she asked.

"Gee, and I thought I was hiding the shakes so well."

She laughed. "Seriously, McCade. Harcourt's flying his Cessna up to the canyon. James is going with him, and they invited me and a cameraman along. It's a great photo op—"

"*You're* going to fly in a *Cessna?*" McCade was astonished, and rightly so. Sandy usually didn't fly in large commercial jets, let alone tiny private airplanes.

"It's a *great* photo op," she said again, trying to convince herself as well. "I was counting on you being there for moral support, but if you can't hold a camera steady—"

"I'll be fine."

"I can ask O'Reilly to do it."

"I *will* be fine."

Sandy's intercom beeped and Laura's voice said, "Mr. Vandenberg is here to review the footage from the shopping mall."

Sandy pushed the intercom button. "Tell him I'll meet him in the editing room."

"That sounds like my cue to leave." He stood up and put her car keys into his pocket. "Thanks for coming to get me last night."

"Thanks for knowing you were too drunk to drive."

McCade shook his head. "I'm afraid I can't take credit for that. The bartender's the one you should thank."

"Then thank him for me." Sandy crossed to the door and reached for the doorknob, but he put his hand against the smooth wood, holding it closed.

"I should kiss you good-bye," he said.

Sandy's heart did a quick three-sixty. "We're alone, McCade. What's the point?"

He gently touched her face. "You don't look like a woman who's been kissed. Vandenberg's going to notice that."

"That's silly," she said weakly, but she didn't move, couldn't move as his mouth found hers.

It was a sweet kiss, gentle and soft, but laced with the same fire that had burned fiercely between them last night. Sandy remembered the way McCade had touched her, the feel of his hand on her breast.

He pulled away. "Now you can go." He nodded in satisfaction. "Now you look kissed."

Sandy pulled open the door. "We're leaving for the airport at four-thirty," she said briskly, to cover her embarrassment. "Pack enough clothes for several days and get back here. Don't be late."

McCade's quiet chuckle followed her down the corridor.

She caught a glimpse of herself in the mirror across from the elevators and stopped short. McCade was right. She *did* look kissed. Her eyes were bright, her face slightly flushed, her cheeks rosy, and her lips . . .

If one little kiss could make her look like this, how had she looked last night, after the two of them had tried to inhale each other in the front seat of her car? Thank God he couldn't remember, because if he did, he would surely realize that she was in love with him.

Turning away from the mirror, she hurried toward the editing room.

As McCade stopped at a red light something reflected from the floor, catching his eye. Another button—the third one he'd found since he'd gotten into Sandy's car.

"Whadidya find?" Frank asked idly as McCade's fingers closed around it.

"Nothing." He slipped it into the ashtray with the other buttons.

That was when the memory hit, slamming into him like a sledgehammer. It was fragmented, in pieces like a jigsaw puzzle, but there were enough to complete the picture. Sandy. McCade. Sitting in this very car. The eerie glow of predawn. Desire exploding inside of him as he kissed her. Buttons exploding off of her shirt as he roughly ripped it open—

"Mercy," he muttered, holding tightly to the steering wheel.

"Light's green," Frank said.

McCade woodenly put the car into gear and drove through the intersection. What had he done? And why hadn't Sandy said anything?

Sandy was sitting in an aluminum soda can with wings that was floating thousands and thousands of feet above the earth.

"What do you say," McCade whispered into her ear, "in order to get some really good shots of Arizona from this altitude, I climb out on the wing and—"

"No!" she said before she realized he was teasing.

"Then I'm done shooting for a while." He grinned at her and carefully set his camera down.

Harcourt was talking on the radio to the tower at the airport near the canyon, and James was in the other front seat reading his mail.

McCade slipped his arm around Sandy, pulling her close. "How're you doing?" he asked quietly.

Sandy could see concern in his eyes and she made herself smile. It was shaky, but it was a smile. "Great," she lied. Takeoff had been the worst. With McCade filming, she'd had no hand to hold, no fingers to squeeze. But he was trying to make up for that now.

"This plane is actually very safe," he whispered into her ear. "You know we would have been at greater risk driving on the highway, and I'm not even talking about riding my Harley. I'm talking about driving a car. Hell, riding a bike would damn near quadruple the risk."

"Thanks for telling me," she muttered. "Now I'll be scared to death whenever you ride your motorcycle."

"I'm always very careful when I ride."

"Careful people wear helmets," she pointed out.

"It's hard to look cool with a helmet on."

"It's even harder to look cool when you're dead."

"Point and game," he conceded with a crooked grin.

His jean-clad thigh was pressed against hers, and he wore one of his standard black T-shirts underneath the bright red shell jacket Sandy had ordered him from the L. L. Bean catalog. He would have been more comfortable in his black leather jacket—she knew he wore this one for her.

Somehow, in the hours between the time he'd appeared in her office late that morning and the four-thirty ride to the airport, McCade had lost that sick, recently-hit-by-a-truck, hungover look. With the exception of slightly bloodshot eyes, she wouldn't have known from looking that he had stayed up until dawn, drinking himself to the point of memory loss.

He smiled at her again, his eyes warm, his lean face creased with laugh lines. Sandy loved his face. Inwardly, she shook her head, admonishing herself. True, he was outrageously handsome, but there was more about McCade to love than just his face. Yeah, there was his body too . . . she snickered to herself as she remembered how wonderful it felt to dance with him, how great it was to have him hold her in his arms.

Still, James was handsome too. James also had a great body. But she didn't love James, she loved McCade.

She loved McCade's tough, streetwise attitude. She loved his quick sense of humor and his gentle kindness. She loved his fierce sense of loyalty, and his smart-aleck mouth that was equally able to get him both into and out of trouble. She loved his keen intelligence and sharp wit. She even loved all the things about him that normally drove her crazy—his overprotectiveness, his inability to keep from taking sides, the chip he still carried on his shoulder from all those years he was dumped on in middle school and high school, his attachment to the open road, and his aversion to settling down.

"This is what it feels like to be a bird," McCade said. "Free and alive, and with an entirely different perspective of the world from the creatures that live on the ground."

He might've been describing himself. Impulsively, she turned and kissed him lightly on the mouth.

McCade was shocked. He had never, not in a million years, expected Sandy to kiss him. Not while they were sitting in the back of a tiny airplane with her two most important clients in the front seat. No way.

But she had. For the first time since she had pushed him away in the movie theater, McCade allowed himself to hope that she could fall in love with him.

But then he frowned, remembering that disturbing memory he had of ripping her shirt open, buttons flying everywhere. Man, he wished he knew what had happened last night. He didn't doubt that he'd been stupid—he was particularly good at that. He just wanted to know exactly how stupid he'd been.

"This isn't so bad." Sandy looked out the window at the mountains that seemed like a relief map so far below them. "You're right about the perspective. Life makes more sense from this altitude. Everything that seems so huge down on the ground is really just laughably small, isn't it?" She leaned back, resting her head against his shoulder. "Flying's really not so bad. I could get used to this."

❖──────────❖

Simon Harcourt took a separate car from the airport to his cabin, leaving James Vandenberg to drive Sandy and McCade to the motel. The technical crew of Video Enterprises was already waiting in the restaurant next to the motel when they arrived.

It was almost eight o'clock, and Sandy was nearly dizzy from fatigue and lack of food. McCade and James followed her into the restaurant, where they joined the crew. After ordering a quick dinner, she made sure everyone had the next day's shooting schedule. If the weather allowed, they'd be hiking part of the way into the canyon with Simon Harcourt and his family. In that case, there would be a six A.M. wake-up call.

"What if it rains?" someone asked.

Sandy smiled. "Then Frank will let you sleep late. If it's raining, we'll meet here at noon for lunch, see what we can do with the afternoon—maybe get some interior shots of Harcourt's cabin."

As she ate the bowl of soup and salad that she'd ordered, the crew straggled out of the restaurant, some of them heading to their rooms across the parking lot in the motel, others heading to the dark little bar that adjoined the restaurant.

McCade and James had ordered hamburgers, and they'd both finished eating while Sandy spoke to the crew. James excused himself, checking on the election-campaign volunteers who'd come to help with all of the little details of the shoot.

Sandy looked up to find McCade watching her. "Do me a favor?" she asked.

He nodded.

"Go over to the motel and check us both in."

He pushed his chair back from the table. "Sure."

Sandy finished her soup and salad then signed the check. She had just climbed tiredly to her feet and was about to hoist her overnight bag onto her shoulder when McCade reappeared. He took her bag in one hand, his bag in the other, and led her out of the restaurant into the parking lot. "Hey, Sandy?"

"No, McCade," she said firmly. "That 'Hey, Sandy' sounded an awful lot like the precursor to bad news, and to tell you the truth, I'm too tired to hear it. Whatever it is, it can wait till the morning." She looked at the numbered doors lining the long, two-story L-shaped motel. "What room am I in?"

"Two thirty-eight."

That meant it was on the top floor. Good. There would be no tourists stomping around over her head at all hours of the night. And number 238 was down on the side of the L directly across the parking lot from the restaurant. It was near a stairwell too. She headed for her motel room, for her nice, clean motel-room bed, her soft motel-room pillow, and deep, oblivious sleep.

McCade was just a step behind her. "What room are *you* in?" she asked over her shoulder.

"Two thirty-eight."

It took about four more steps, but the meaning of what McCade said finally penetrated her consciousness. She stopped walking and turned to face him.

"That's what I was trying to tell you," he told her apologetically.

She turned and looked toward the motel office, but he shook his head, anticipating her next move.

"I already tried, but they're booked solid, there's no other room available. I had them call the motel down the road, but they're filled up too. I even tried the lodges out in the national park, but the people in the reservations office out there just laughed at me. If you want, I could squeeze in with Frank and O'Reilly."

She closed her eyes. "I'm going to *kill* Laura."

"Laura?"

"She made these reservations." She opened her eyes and looked at McCade. "Even if we really *were* involved, McCade, unless we were married, we wouldn't go on a business trip and share a room. It's just not professional. It looks so . . . sleazy."

McCade shifted the weight of the bags in his hands. "Let me carry your stuff to the room, then I'll try to find Frank—"

"And sleep on the floor?" She shook her head. "No, look, McCade, we can share a room. We just have to be discreet. It's not *that* big a deal anyway. It's not really that different from you staying in my condo with me, right?"

He didn't answer, so she went on. "Motel rooms usually have two beds. You can take one bed, I'll take the other, and everything will work out fine. Okay?"

She was trying to convince herself as much as McCade. Sharing a motel room with him really wasn't anything like sharing her condo. In her condo, she could escape into another room when her feelings started becoming too intense, when her attraction to him started pulling her in his direction. But this was for just a few nights, she told herself firmly. Surely she could go for a few nights without throwing herself at the man. Couldn't she?

Silently, McCade followed her up the stairs to room number 238. He watched as Sandy put the key into the lock and opened the door. She flipped on the lights as they went in and—

Sandy swore softly.

One bed.

The room had only one king-size bed.

McCade stepped inside, pushing the door shut with his foot. He dropped his own bag on the floor near the door, but set hers on the dresser. "I'll go find Frank."

"Wait."

The energy he'd found to shoot this evening's plane ride had drained him, and he looked exhausted. "I gotta keep moving, or I'm going to fall down," he told her when she didn't continue.

"What if you can't find Frank?"

"I'll crash in one of the vans."

"It gets cold up here at night," she said. "We're in the mountains, remember?" She took a deep breath, letting it out in a loud burst. "This is a big bed. And we're grown-ups. We can share it, right?"

McCade shook his head. "I don't know, Sand."

"You can't sleep on the floor in Frank's room," she said decisively. "It would look too weird. Everyone thinks we're living together. And I *definitely* don't want you sleeping in the van. Maybe tomorrow they'll have another room."

He shook his head again. "They're booked solid through the weekend."

"Maybe someone will call and cancel." She sat on the bed and pulled off her boots, tossing them next to the wall. "I'm going to take a shower and then go to sleep. We have to get up early in the morning."

She rummaged in her bag, pulling out one of her little cotton nightgowns. She tucked it under her arm as she started unbuttoning her shirt.

Buttons. In his mind, McCade saw buttons flying through the air inside of Sandy's little car. He saw

Sandy, so beautiful and sexy, her eyes filled with desire. . . .

He turned away, suddenly painfully aware of his rock-solid desire. He'd been walking around in a state of confusion for weeks now, ever since he'd arrived on Sandy's doorstep, and the thought of sharing that enormous bed with her had pushed him over the top.

Mercy, he wanted her.

And if that memory he had of ripping her shirt open really was a memory and not a dream, then he was seriously out of control. What was he thinking, *if?* That was no dream. The buttons he'd found in her car were proof of that.

He heard the sound of the water go on, and slowly took off his jacket.

He was next in line for a shower—a *very* cold one.

"Hey, Sandy?"

McCade's voice came from the darkness on the other side of the bed. She rolled onto her side, trying to get comfortable. The mattress had seen better days, though, and McCade's weight on one end made it seem as if she were sleeping on the side of a hill.

"Yeah?" she answered.

"This is sorta strange, you know?"

Oh, yeah. She knew. "Close your eyes, McCade. If you're even *half* as tired as I am, you'll fall asleep right away."

"I'm sorry. It's my fault that you're so tired."

"Remember that the next time you go out drinking. I haven't lectured you yet, have I?"

"Nope."

Sandy turned to face him. "There are more ways to

die from drinking than drunk driving," she told him sternly. "You could have overdosed and died from alcohol poisoning."

"You know, I didn't go out intending to get skunked," he said. "When I left your place, I didn't plan to drink at all."

"So why did you?"

He didn't answer right away, and the darkness pressed down on Sandy mercilessly. She longed to see his face, see his eyes, know what he was thinking.

"I got drunk because riding my bike didn't help," he finally said.

Riding his bike didn't . . . ? Disappointment clutched at her. He was feeling tied down, and she knew what she had to do. She had to set him free. "You don't have to stay." She hoped he couldn't hear the tightness in her throat, suddenly glad for the darkness that kept him from seeing her face. "After this weekend I can replace you, even with just a few hours' notice. So don't stick around out of a sense of guilt. If you have to go, I can get along without you."

Her words echoed in the darkness. She could get along without him. Of course she could.

McCade lay in silence, seeing buttons shooting through the air. Oh, man, did she *want* him to leave? He couldn't ask. He cleared his throat, but he couldn't find the words to ask her what had happened last night. But he was dying to know. Had he kissed her? Had he tried to make love to her? What had he said, and how had she answered?

Not for the first time since he'd awakened that morning, he cursed his inability to remember.

Heat. He saw it in Sandy's eyes, felt it in her touch, tasted it on her lips. She drew him toward her, and as their mouths met again there was an explosion of fire.

Their clothes fell away, dissolving around them, and he was touching her. Sweet Lord, he'd waited so long for this. Her legs opened, she was ready for him, and he couldn't wait. He entered her almost savagely and she cried out, her voice thick with pleasure.

But suddenly she pushed him away.

Then he was sitting in Sandy's car. They were both fully dressed, and Sandy was crying.

But as suddenly as she had started to cry, she stopped.

If you still want to make love to me when you're sober— Sandy watched him steadily—*just let me know, okay?*

McCade sat up in the darkness of the motel room. His heart was pounding, and the sound of his breathing, unsteady and ragged seemed to rattle around him. He ran his hands down his face. Talk about vivid dreams. This one had been so realistic that—

He shook his head. No. It couldn't be. Could it?

His heart rate had finally returned to normal, but the thought that Sandy might actually have said those words to him made it kick into overdrive again. But then he frowned. Part of that dream had to be just that—a dream.

It was his recurrent fantasy—she was in his bed and she wanted him to make love to her. But that other stuff, the words she had spoken right before he woke up, that was new.

Sandy was asleep a short distance away from him.

He didn't want to wake her. Lord knows he'd kept her up enough last night. But he did want to hold her.

Gently he eased his arms around her, molding his body around hers, tucking her head underneath his chin.

He'd talk to her in the morning. Maybe it would rain, and they wouldn't have to get out of bed at the crack of dawn. She'd wake up with his arms around her, and he would tell her that he was sober, and watch for her reaction.

Sandy sighed, and McCade closed his eyes. Breathing in her sweet scent, holding her tightly, he fell back into a deep sleep.

The phone was ringing relentlessly, invading the soft warmth of Sandy's dreams. At last she could ignore it no longer, and she opened her eyes.

McCade's eyes opened a fraction of a second later, and Sandy stared into their swirling mix of colors as he gazed at her, confusion clearly written on his face.

They were nose to nose, and her arm was wrapped possessively around his neck, her legs tangled casually with his.

She pulled away from him, blushing furiously, thinking, God, she'd gone and done it. She'd damn near forced herself on him in the night. She rolled over so that her back was to him as she answered the telephone, thankful for a chance to hide her warm cheeks. "Kirk."

"Morning, boss," came Frank's cheerful voice. "It's six o'clock. Rise and shine. God's on our side. We've got fifty-five degrees and sunshine. Remember to dress in layers, it'll get hotter as we go down into the canyon."

"Thanks, Frank."

"Oh, boss? Clint McCade's not on my room list," he said. "I'm assuming you know where he is?"

Sandy closed her eyes briefly. "Yeah," she said. Yes,

she certainly did know where McCade was. He was hardly even an arm's distance from her, looking too good for words with his rumpled hair and the stubble of beard on his handsome face.

"Great," Frank said. "See you in a few."

Pushing her tangled hair back from her face, she hung up the phone. With her back to McCade, she climbed out of bed.

"Sandy."

She turned around to find him watching her, his head propped up on one arm. His eyes were serious, his expression almost somber. "We have to talk."

Her heart sank. He was going to tell her that after this weekend he was leaving. She'd given her feelings away by throwing herself into his arms last night, and now he had a better reason to leave than ever.

But she didn't want to hear that right now. She didn't want to spend her entire day knowing he would soon be gone.

"Not right now, McCade." She tried to keep her voice light as she headed toward the bathroom. "If we don't get a move on, we'll miss breakfast. And trust me, we don't want to hike down into the Grand Canyon without breakfast."

She closed the bathroom door tightly behind her, and McCade exhaled the breath he'd been holding. Damn. She was right, though. There was work to do today, and now wasn't the right time for a heart-to-heart, particularly when his heart was filled with so many secrets.

NINE

Sandy shook Simon Harcourt's hand as they congratulated each other on a good day's work, then she hopped up into the equipment van. Everything was loaded and ready to go back to the motel at the entrance to the park.

The sun was setting, and after nearly twelve hours of sweat and dust and merciless heat, Sandy was ready for a shower and a cold glass of beer—not necessarily in that order.

Frank hopped in behind the steering wheel, tossing his clipboard between the two front seats.

"Everyone accounted for?" Sandy asked.

"Yep." The young man pushed his glasses higher up on his thin nose. He glanced in the rearview mirror, then frowned. "I mean, no. Where's McCade? I thought he was with you."

"It's not like we're Siamese twins, Frank," she said crossly. "We're not attached at the hip."

"Hips weren't what I was thinking." Frank had a wicked twinkle in his eyes. "Permission to speak freely, boss?"

"Since when have you started asking for permission?"

"McCade tells me I need to work on being tactful. So I'm trying to be tactful. You giving me permission, or what?"

"Fire away."

"The truth is, you're a real babe," he said earnestly. "And McCade's nuts about you. I mean, you'd have to be blind not to notice the way he looks at you."

Indeed. And Sandy was far from blind. All day long she'd been aware of McCade's hot eyes following her around. But it was all part of this game they were playing, the "fool James Vandenberg into thinking they really were lovers" game. Unfortunately, her crew was being fooled along with James.

"And at the risk of being tactless," Frank went on, "I have to confess that I caught you looking at McCade pretty much the same way."

Guilty as charged. She *had* looked at McCade, she couldn't deny it. She hadn't been able to keep her eyes away from him, particularly as the day got hotter and he stripped off his T-shirt. He'd set up his shots, sometimes moving quickly down the trail ahead of them, with his heavy camera on his shoulder, the muscles in his bare back and arms rippling. And Sandy had ogled him, thinking no one would notice.

"I really think you guys should get married," Frank said.

Married. Right. "Thanks for the advice, Frank."

"You guys are perfect for each other."

Yeah, they were perfect all right. McCade was a perfect actor, and Sandy was a perfect fool.

"Where *is* McCade?" she muttered. "I'm starving and thirsty and—"

She and Frank spotted him at the same time.

He was at the edge of the Grand Canyon with his camera, shooting the brilliant sunset. Sandy opened the door and slid down, out of the van. "I'll be right back."

But she walked slowly as she approached McCade, struck by the beauty of his solitary, shadowy figure standing against a backdrop of blazing colors.

He lowered his camera as she came and stood beside him, but he didn't look toward her. He gazed out at the breathtaking vista.

"It's so beautiful," he said quietly. "It doesn't seem quite real."

Sandy nodded. "To me it always looks like a matte painting, like a special effect. I think my brain refuses to accept that nature could have created something that huge—or that perfect."

"It *is* perfect, isn't it?" McCade laughed, shaking his head and turning to look down at her. "Maybe that's what scares me so much about the damned thing. It's perfect, except I don't believe in perfection. So I don't trust it. I think I keep waiting for it to just melt away, to vanish, you know?"

She gazed up at him. His hair was disheveled and damp with sweat at the back of his neck. The hot desert sun had darkened his tan another shade, and his eyes seemed very blue in contrast. He still had his shirt off, and his muscular chest was covered with a fine layer of trail dust.

"Yeah, I know." She turned back to the waiting van. "Come on, McCade, I'll buy you a beer."

"No, thanks. No beer for me. I still haven't recovered from two nights ago."

"Then I'll buy you a soda."

McCade wanted her to wait. He wanted to use this

opportunity to mention that he was sober. He wanted to see how she would react, see if she caught the implication, see if she really did say those words he was so afraid he'd only dreamed. *If you still want to make love to me when you're sober, just let me know.*

"Sandy—" he started, but she had already climbed into the van. Frank was in the driver's seat, and the chance to talk was gone.

Tonight, McCade thought as he packed his camera into the van. At some point tonight, they'd be alone. Then maybe he'd get up enough nerve to tell her how he felt. His worst-case scenario had her looking at him with pity in her pretty eyes. Then he'd find some excuse to leave at the end of the weekend, take his Harley and go off somewhere and live unhappily ever after with wounded pride and a broken heart. Best-case scenario . . .

McCade smiled as Frank drove down the long road that led out of the national park.

"What's the joke?" she asked.

He just shook his head.

"Whoa," McCade said, looking pointedly at the several empty beer mugs that sat in front of Sandy's steak. "Baby, you better slow down."

She lifted her eyebrows as he slid into the chair next to hers in the motel saloon. She raised her voice to be heard over the jukebox. "What's this? A temperance lecture from Mr. Inebriation?"

"You have the opportunity to learn from my mistakes." He dug into his own dinner. His hair was still wet from the quick shower he'd taken when they'd returned to the motel. "You don't normally drink two mugs of beer, let alone four. Keep it up, and I'm going to have to carry you out of here."

Sandy opened her mouth to tell McCade that three of the empty mugs in front of her had held nothing but water, but stopped. Let him believe what he wanted. She was tired and frustrated and dreading returning to that sole bed in their motel room.

She let the music wash over her, trying not to think.

Someone had pulled several tables together to form one long one, and the crew of Video Enterprises sat around it.

She could feel McCade watching her as he ate, so she pretended to be fascinated by the rustic saloon.

The interior decorator had clearly chosen darkness for financial rather than aesthetic reasons. The walls were plain, rough-hewn planks, and the floors were well-worn wood—or at least they would be in the light of day or with the dim overhead lights turned up to full power. As it was, even with the dusky light coming in through the big window that covered the front, she could barely make out either the walls or the floors. Booths lined one wall, a long polished wood bar lined another. There was a jukebox off to one side—a beacon of light in the cavernous darkness. Sandy wouldn't have noticed it if it weren't for the machine's blinking lights—and the country music that was pounding out of it. Nearby, a small portion of the floor was reserved for dancing.

From the corner of her eye, she saw McCade push his plate away and lean back in his seat. He slipped his arm around her shoulders and leaned close to her ear. "James just came in."

Sandy glanced up. Sure enough. There was James, standing by the bar, talking to several people she recognized as campaign volunteers.

She looked at McCade, and for a brief instant she felt totally off balance, thrown by the heat of his eyes. But then he smiled, a junior version of his crooked, cocky grin, and she felt a sudden flash of anger. She was tired of this game. She didn't want to play anymore.

She stood abruptly, and his arm fell away from her. "Excuse me." She took her collection of beer mugs to the bar.

In a few days McCade was going to leave. As afraid as she was that he would never come back if he knew that she loved him, Sandy realized she was more afraid of letting him go without telling him how she felt. Or showing him how she felt. Yeah, *showing* him.

She felt his eyes on her as she ordered another beer. He thought it was her fourth, while it was really just her second. Good, she thought with almost childish satisfaction. Let him think that. Maybe if she played her cards right, he *would* carry her out of the bar. The rules of this game have changed, she thought, turning to meet his watchful gaze. Maybe he was going to leave, but he wasn't going to leave until she got a chance to show him just what he was going to be missing.

"Cassandra." James smiled at her, propping one elbow on the bar. "It went well today, don't you think?"

She forced herself to stop thinking about McCade, to smile up at James. "Yeah, I do. I'll know for sure when I see the footage we got."

"What's the plan for tomorrow?" he asked.

"Howdy, James."

Sandy looked up to see McCade standing beside her. He, too, was leaning against the bar, but with his arm outstretched behind her. Although he wasn't touching her, his position was obviously proprietary.

James nodded pleasantly. "McCade."

Sandy took a sip of her beer, turning back to James as if their conversation hadn't been interrupted. "We'll go out to the Harcourts' cabin and get some outside footage, maybe stage a little family cookout."

"I heard a weather report," James told her, making a face. "We might get some rain tonight. It's supposed to last until late morning."

"Then we'll have to play tomorrow by ear," she said.

"Honey, could I have a slug of your beer?" McCade didn't wait for her to answer; he just took the mug from her hand and drained the glass.

Honey? Sandy stared in disbelief at the empty glass he handed back to her. "McCade—"

"Let's dance." He took the mug from her again and set it on the bar. "You'll excuse us, won't you, James?" He pulled her onto the dance floor over by the jukebox.

"You drank my entire beer!" Sandy's voice rose with indignation. "I thought you weren't going to drink tonight."

"I figured you already had enough."

His arms held her tightly, and Sandy resisted for all of a half second before giving up and relaxing. She was exactly where she wanted to be—in McCade's arms—so why was she fighting it?

But then she noticed that the Video Enterprises table was empty. "Hey, where did the crew go?"

"There's a honky-tonk with a live band about forty-five minutes down the road," McCade told her. "They wanted us to come with them, but I figured you wouldn't want to."

"You could've at least asked," Sandy said accusingly. "Why didn't you?"

McCade grabbed at the easiest excuse. "Because James is here." Truth was, he still wanted a chance to talk to her alone, even though it was likely she'd already had too much to drink to have a serious conversation.

"How's my body language now?" Sandy asked, smiling grimly up at him. Her eyes narrowed slightly as he gazed back at her.

"You look like you're mad at me," he finally said.

She pulled her hand free from his. Reaching up around his neck, she locked her hands together. The movement brought her closer to him, and her body brushed his chest. Lightly, with her thumb, she stroked the back of his neck.

"Better?" she asked.

"Sandy, this isn't—"

She interrupted him by pulling his head down and rising on tiptoe to cover his mouth with her own.

McCade hesitated for all of two seconds before surrendering. She kissed him slowly, lazily, and quite thoroughly.

"How's *that* for body language?" Sandy tried to act casually, but her voice had an out-of-breath quality to it.

McCade's voice sounded strange too. "You better watch out. I'm not sure you're aware of the message you're sending."

James. It always came back to James. But not any longer, Sandy thought. Not anymore.

"James already thinks you live with me," she told McCade. "He's hardly going to be shocked to see me kiss you. Besides, didn't you once make some kind of comment about how everybody always wants to play with the other kid's toys?" She purposely dropped her gaze to his mouth, to those lips that could kiss her so fabulously, lips that could make her feel so utterly consumed by both her own passion—and his.

Somehow McCade managed to keep dancing. She'd

misunderstood him, assuming he was worried about what James would think. In truth, he'd been talking about himself. Be careful of the message you're giving to *me* was what he'd meant.

And now she was looking at him, giving him signals that said she wanted him to kiss her. But why? Because James was here, watching? Because she wanted to practice sending messages via body language? Or because she actually wanted McCade to kiss her?

He could only dare to hope, but dare he did.

As Sandy met his gaze he searched the depths of her eyes, looking for something that would tell him this wasn't just part of the game. He saw desire, hot and liquid, but he also saw uncertainty. She was unsure of herself, doubtful of her appeal, afraid he wouldn't want her. And every moment that he hesitated, every second longer that he didn't kiss her, that uncertainty grew.

And McCade couldn't bear that.

He kissed her hard, crushing his mouth to hers, catching her by surprise and pulling her with him into one of the deserted corners of the bar.

Sandy wasn't even aware that they were moving until her back hit the wall. And still McCade kept coming, still he kissed her, still he tried to get closer to her.

One of his hands was laced through her hair, holding her head as he kept kissing her. His long, intimate kisses sent arrows of fire shooting through her body, through her blood, to land molten and burning deep within her.

His other hand encircled her hips, roughly pulling her even closer to him. Oh God, she felt the unmistakable hard length of his erection pressing against her stomach. He wanted her. McCade wanted her. Sandy kissed him fiercely, nearly delirious with the knowledge.

She moved her hips, rubbing herself against him and

McCade groaned, a low, sexy sound of need and desire and she nearly laughed out loud. Oh yeah, he wanted her.

McCade's head was spinning. Damn, he couldn't take much more of this. Here in the dark corner of the bar they were shadows—two shadows merged into one. He could kiss her in the privacy the darkness provided. But kissing her wasn't enough. He wanted to touch her. He wanted to rip off her clothes, rid them both of the barriers that kept him from her.

But he knew there were bigger barriers between them than the clothes they wore. They needed to talk. But when he pulled back, Sandy kissed him again, slipping her hands up under the edge of his T-shirt. The sensation of her fingers against his hot skin made him gasp. He heard her breathless laughter as she ran her hands up his back, as she wrapped one of her legs around his own.

"Sandy . . ." he whispered. Oh man, he could feel the heat between her legs against his thigh, even through his jeans. Did she know what she was doing to him? How much had she had to drink? Nearly four mugs of beer, he remembered, closing his eyes in despair. She'd had way too much to drink. Dammit, this wasn't fair. "We can't stay here like this."

"Then let's leave."

McCade saw the white flash of her smile as she took his hand and pulled him toward the door.

No, that wasn't what he'd meant. He wanted to sit down in one of the booths, with the safety of a wooden table between them. That table would keep him from pulling her back into his arms. He wanted to sit there and talk—try to talk, see if she was able to talk.

"Baby, wait."

But she didn't slow down until they were both outside the heavy glass door, until they were standing on the wooden porch of the restaurant.

The night air was cool and smelled like the pine trees that surrounded the area. Sandy took a deep breath, clearing her lungs of the secondhand smoke that had hung like a cloud in the bar. McCade still held her hand and his palm was damp. Holy cow, had she made Clint McCade sweat? She turned to look at him and saw a bead of perspiration run down one of his sideburns, past his ear. She had. She smiled. She'd actually made him sweat.

"Sandy." McCade's voice was raspier than ever, and he cleared his throat, started again. "You know, I think that—"

"McCade, just kiss me." She didn't want him to think. She didn't want him to wonder, she didn't want him to analyze where this all would lead. There'd be plenty of time to think after they got there.

Lit by the dim streetlights that were spaced throughout the parking lot, McCade's face was shadowed and mysterious.

Sandy felt light-headed. She couldn't believe she was actually planning to seduce McCade. But she was. If she could just get him off the porch, across the parking lot, up those stairs, and into the privacy of their room, he wasn't going to know what hit him. And then, she thought almost grimly, *then* when he left town, at least she'd know that she'd given it her best shot, that she'd let him know how she felt.

McCade was still watching her. What she would have given to get inside his head. All she knew was, he wanted her. She could see his desire on his face and in the way he stood with one hand jammed into his front pocket, as if he was trying to hide the telltale bulge in the front of his jeans.

Yes, he wanted her. And knowing that gave her downward-spiraling self-confidence a much-needed boost.

"Come on," she whispered, tugging gently at his hand, trying to draw him toward her. "Kiss me again."

"Why?"

Sandy stared at him, caught in the intensity of his gaze. *Because I love you.* But she couldn't bring herself to say those words.

"James is watching," she said instead, motioning toward the glass windows of the bar, taking the coward's way out.

It wasn't the answer McCade wanted, and he looked away from her before she could see the disappointment in his eyes.

James. The man was a little too stiff, a little too straitlaced, but basically a nice guy. Still, at that moment, McCade couldn't recall disliking anyone more.

He felt Sandy slip her arms around his neck and he groaned. *Sandy, don't do this to me.* He never got the chance to say the words aloud—she stood on her toes and pressed her lips against his before he could speak.

McCade didn't stand a chance. He closed his eyes and kissed her, losing himself in the lightning bolt of emotion that ripped through him. Damn, he loved her. He felt tears sting his eyelids and he wanted to push her away, to shout, to yell, to stomp his feet and beg her not to use him this way. But he also wanted to kiss her, to keep on kissing her, to let her do with him whatever she damn well pleased.

So he kissed her. And kissed her and kissed her, matching her passion and hunger, praying he'd be able to back off when she asked him to, praying she wouldn't ask.

Through a haze of desire, McCade realized that somehow they'd moved off the porch and across the parking lot to the foot of the motel stairwell. Sandy tugged at his hand, turning to lead him up the steps, but he wanted to kiss her again. Catching her around the waist, he pulled her against him. He loved her. He loved her, dammit, and the time to tell her was long overdue. He swept his tongue into her mouth, tasting her, invading her, surrendering to the feelings he'd kept hidden from her for so many weeks.

He knew in a flash of desperate hope exactly what he had to do. He had to take her upstairs, up to the privacy of their room, and tell her the truth. If she'd had too much to drink and couldn't understand, he'd put her to bed, let her sleep it off. But then he'd tell her in the morning. First thing. Regardless of the six A.M. wake-up call. Regardless of the morning's shooting schedule.

Sandy had molded her body to his, and McCade nearly choked as she pressed herself against his arousal. Lord have mercy, she knew he was hot for her, he thought, instantly realizing just how inane an observation that was. Of course she knew. Damn, he had a hard-on the size of Alaska. She was *bound* to have noticed.

But she was kissing him again and rubbing herself against him—her body language was unmistakable.

With a strangled groan, he swung her into his arms. He took the stairs two at a time, and was at the top in an instant.

Sandy's heart was hammering as McCade gently set her down outside the door to their room. Suddenly afraid of what she'd see in his eyes, she kept her arms wrapped around his neck, pulling his mouth down toward hers for yet another kiss. Even as he kissed her she felt him dig in his pockets for the room key, and heard the bolt click as he unlocked it.

The door swung open and they were inside, and McCade was looking at her in the muted light.

Although he hadn't moved away from her, although he was still holding her, Sandy could tell that mentally he had taken a step back.

The door was closed, the curtains drawn, and unless James Vandenberg had X-ray vision, there was no way on earth she could use him as an excuse. McCade released her, and she knew she had no choice. She'd have to tell the truth.

He moved away from her, his lean face unsmiling.

Now. She had to say it now.

Sandy took a step forward, following him, keeping them close together. She took a deep breath. "What would you do if I asked you not to stop?"

He froze, and she took another step toward him. They were inches apart, close enough to kiss, close enough for her to feel his body heat. But he didn't reach out, didn't touch her. He looked into her eyes, though, and the connection between them was nearly palpable.

"I guess I'd have to ask you why." He spoke slowly, carefully. "Unless you could give me a damn good reason why we shouldn't stop, I'd have to assume it was the beer talking, and leave it at that."

His eyes were remarkably beautiful. As Sandy looked into them, at the flecks of gold and green that adorned the blue, his gaze flickered for a moment, down to her mouth.

It was just for a second, maybe two, but McCade's unconscious message was clear. Despite his words of caution, he wanted to kiss her.

That awareness gave Sandy the confidence she needed. "Clint." Her voice was barely a whisper, and it shook slightly as she tried to make it louder. "What would a damn good reason be? I mean, can you give me an example . . . ?"

She moistened her lips, and again his gaze dropped to her mouth, this time lingering.

"Yeah," he said huskily. "Like, if you told me that you want me. *Me*, not James. That would be one hell of a damn good reason."

"If that was what I told you," she said, "what would you say then?"

McCade closed his eyes briefly, and when he opened them he looked directly at her. "I love you, Sandy," he whispered. "I'd tell you that I'm in love with you."

He loved her. Clint loved her. Sandy could barely breathe. She had to concentrate to draw air into her lungs, to push it back out.

"And then," he added softly, "if you could convince me that you didn't have too much to drink, if I could be sure that you really know what you're doing, I'd take your hand and lead you over to that bed and I'd make love to you."

Sandy stared into McCade's eyes for many long seconds, as his words seemed to echo in the room. *I'd make love to you.*

The seconds stretched nearly into a minute before she realized he was waiting for her to say something. It was her turn, her move.

"I only had one beer," she told him.

McCade frowned. "But—"

"I had all those beer mugs on the table," she answered before he could even ask. "But most of 'em held water. I'm sober. How about you?"

*If you still want to make love to me when you're sober, just
let me know.*

Their eyes met. "It wasn't a dream, was it?"

Sandy shook her head no.

"I'm sober too." He grinned, a quick nervous flash of
white teeth against his tanned face. "Lord, I don't think
I've ever been more sober in my entire life."

"Then . . . don't stop," she whispered. "Make love
to me, Clint."

"Why?" McCade asked her, just as he said he would.

Sandy looked down at herself, saw the way she was
standing, and frowned slightly. She relaxed her arms and
held out her hands to McCade, palms up. "Because I
want you. Because I love you."

He took a step toward her, and then another, and
Sandy met him halfway. She caught her breath, amazed
at the sight of tears shining in his eyes as he took her in
his arms. He kissed her, not fiercely, the way she expected, but tenderly, slowly, as if he had all the time in
the world.

"And I love you." He kissed her again, long, deep,
unhurried kisses that made the room seem to tilt around
her.

His hands were gentle as he unfastened the buttons
on her blouse. The tips of his fingers brushed lightly
against her bare skin, pushing the soft cotton back, tugging the shirt free from the waistband of her shorts.

"This is weird." Sandy shook her head. "I know you
so well, but, God—"

"It *is* weird," McCade agreed. "Wonderfully weird."

Her braid had long since come undone. He kissed
her again and slid his fingers through her hair.

Taking her by the hand, he led her to the bed. Letting go, he pulled off his T-shirt and tossed it onto the floor.

"Do you remember the time I got that fishhook in my foot?" Sandy asked suddenly.

She could see surprise in McCade's eyes as he turned to look at her. She sat down on the bed and slipped off her boots, pulling her legs in close to her chest and wrapping her arms tightly around her knees, in an attempt to keep from reaching for him.

With his shirt off, his tanned chest gleamed in the lamplight. The shadows defined his muscles, making him look rugged and strong.

His face relaxed into a smile as he threw himself down next to her on the bed. Almost magically, he turned back into McCade again—McCade, her old buddy, her best friend. The muscles were still there, and the heat of desire still shone from his eyes, but in this relaxed, almost nonchalant pose, the effect he had on her wasn't quite so overwhelming. "It was the summer you turned fourteen. I carried you to the hospital on my back. Three miles. You screamed the entire way."

"I was scared," she said defensively. "It hurt like hell."

McCade propped his head up with one elbow, reaching out his other hand and lightly touching the tips of her toes. "Then when we got home, your mother had a fit, kicked me out, and told me never to come back." He smiled into Sandy's eyes. "At least not until she got over the shock of seeing her poor baby bandaged up."

Sandy looked down at his hand, which still stroked her toes. How could such a seemingly nonintimate touch be so sensual, so sexy? "You snuck up the fire escape to my room that night."

"I was worried about you." He grinned. "The way

your mother was carrying on, I thought you were maybe going to drop dead from tetanus or something. I wanted a chance to apologize before they buried you."

"Do you remember what you told me?" she asked.

He shook his head. "No."

"You said that we should never have gone fishing in the first place. You said that it was a stupid idea, and that my getting hurt was all your fault."

McCade shrugged. "Maybe it wasn't *all* my fault." He gave her a quick smile. "You were the genius who didn't watch where you were walking. But the fact is, if I hadn't had the brilliant idea to go fishing, you never would have been hurt."

"If I hadn't been born, McCade, I never would have been hurt," Sandy said tartly. "It really makes me mad to think that we never tried to fish again."

His hand stilled on her foot, and he frowned down at the bedspread. "I wasn't cut out to be a fisherman, at least not the kind that sits on the end of a pier and waits for a fish to swim by and grab the bait. After you got hurt, it seemed kind of pointless to try again." He glanced up at her searchingly. "Why are we talking about fishing?"

She closed her eyes and answered honestly. "Because I'm stalling. I'm scared."

McCade was quiet for a moment.

"I guess I am too," he finally said. "But it's a good kind of scared. It's a kick, like a roller-coaster ride, you know?"

She knew. But roller-coaster rides always ended too soon.

McCade rolled onto his stomach, reaching for her, pulling her down next to him on the bed. He kissed her sweetly, but that sweetness was laced with passion, intoxicating passion.

Sandy felt herself respond, felt herself cling to him, felt her arms tighten around his neck, as if she was holding on for dear life. A roller-coaster ride, he'd said. She'd always been drawn to roller coasters. But it was a love/hate relationship. She dreaded the thought of that hellish ride up, up, up the tracks. And the first teeth-rattling drop was nothing short of torture. Yet somehow she always found herself coming back for more. . . .

"Sandy, what's wrong?" McCade's soft voice interrupted her thoughts. She opened her eyes to find him looking down at her, his face almost somber. God, he could read her like a book. "We don't have to do this. You know, we can wait."

As she watched him he rolled his eyes and smiled, his grin crooked and so very McCade-like that she had to smile too. "Man, did I really just say that?" he asked. "Who would've believed those words would've ever come out of *this* mouth, huh?" His smile faded, and the sheepish look vanished from his eyes. They turned smoky, luminous, reflecting the hunger she could see on his face. "Truth is, baby, I don't want to wait. I want you. I've never made love before, not the way I want to make it with you." He took a deep breath, exhaling noisily through his mouth. "But if you're not ready for this—"

"Clint, I don't want a one-night stand." The words ran together in her haste to get them out.

He was quiet again, just looking down at her. "When I said that I love you, I meant it," he told her. "I don't want just one night, either. I want forever."

Forever. Sandy stared at him, surprised at his choice of words. Forever? Of course, anything longer than three months was forever to McCade. She wouldn't allow herself to dream that he was referring to anything other than a short-term forever. Still, his words gave her hope that he'd stick around for the summer, maybe even longer, until the lure of the open road finally pulled him away from her.

The bottom line was that when it came to Clint McCade, she'd take what she could get.

She kissed him, pulling him on top of her, opening her legs, bringing him even closer. She heard him groan, a sound that was half pain, half pleasure as he lifted his head to look deep into her eyes.

"I want you to be sure about this," he whispered. "About me."

"I'm sure." She'd never wanted anyone more than she wanted McCade. She was *damn* sure about that. But she was also sure that after he left, she'd spend the rest of her life searching for a man who made her feel half of what she felt right now. And she was sure she'd never find anyone who came remotely close.

But the future was far in the distance.

Sandy smiled. "You know what I'm *not* sure about?"

Silently, he shook his head.

"I'm not sure why we still have our clothes on."

McCade relaxed, a slow smile spreading across his face. "I can take care of that. Unless you want to talk about, oh, say . . . the first time we went bowling?"

She laughed and McCade kissed her possessively, hungrily, his tongue filling her, and her laughter turned to a moan of pleasure.

True to his word, McCade made their clothes disappear. The sensation of his warm body against hers was so much better than anything Sandy had dreamed or imagined. He was hard as steel underneath the sleek smoothness of his tanned skin, and she explored his body with her mouth and hands even as he touched her. His hands were so gentle, and he took his time, caressing her, stroking her. He kissed her breasts, encircling her tender nipples with his tongue, sending fire shooting through her.

She wanted him to fill her body the way he filled her soul. Reaching down, she found him, hard and smooth against her. As her hands surrounded him he groaned and drew harder on her breast. Pleasure tore through her, and she didn't want to wait another minute.

She guided him down, lifting her hips to receive him.

But he pulled back, out of her reach. He kissed her slowly, deliberately, lazily, as his hand moved down, across her flat belly, then even lower. At the first touch of his lightly exploring fingers, she moaned, lifting her hips and pressing herself against his hand. More. She wanted more.

"Please," she breathed. "Clint, please. I need you now."

Her soft words made McCade scramble for his jeans, for his wallet, for the condom he'd put there weeks ago, on the night he'd pointed his Harley east, toward Phoenix and Sandy. Tearing open the small foil package, he sat back on the bed.

Sandy was watching him, lying back against the pillows. Her hair fanned out around her like a golden cloud, and her skin shone in the soft light. He could see the faint outline of a bathing suit she'd worn in the sun. Her breasts were two triangles of creamy, pale skin, the darker pink of her nipples erect, as if waiting for his touch.

Her eyes were half-closed, and as she watched him cover himself she focused on his masculine parts with an interest that made him even harder than he already was. Her gaze flicked up to meet his eyes, and she smiled. It was a smile of anticipation, and it made her beautiful face even more lovely.

"If I wake up in the morning, and this turns out to be just another erotic dream, I'm going to be really depressed," she said.

"Oh, baby. How long have you been having libidinous dreams about me?" McCade teased, crawling across the bed toward her.

Sandy lowered her eyes, as if aware she'd given herself away. "For about a decade or so," she answered honestly.

"All that time . . . ?" he sputtered. "Lord have mercy, Kirk, I never had a clue."

"Of course not." She stretched out her leg, touching his arm lightly with her foot. "I never told you in so many words, and . . . well, you know, back then I was a body-language illiterate."

McCade grinned, his eyes raking over her naked body as he resumed his predatory crawl toward her. "You seem to have overcome your communication problem. Right now I can tell from your body language *exactly* what you're thinking."

Sandy laughed. "I'm lying here without any clothes on. You better know what I'm thinking, or I'm in real trouble."

"You're thinking that you're hungry," he said. "You want to order a pizza and watch Country Music Television."

Sandy hit him with a pillow.

"I was kidding," he protested, grabbing her to keep her from hitting him again.

He had her pinned, her wrists held with one hand,

her arms above her head. He could feel the softness of her breasts and stomach as he looked into her eyes.

"Do you really love me?" Her voice was breathless.

"Yeah," he answered huskily. "I really do. Is that so hard to believe?"

Sandy was quiet for a moment, just gazing up into his eyes. Then she laughed. "Well, yeah, McCade, actually, it is. I may need some convincing."

They were nose to nose, and McCade smiled and then kissed her, losing himself in the sweetness of her mouth. "I love you," he whispered between kisses. "I love you. I love you."

Man, she was so soft, so sweet. Her arms were around his neck, her fingers in his hair as she returned each kiss fiercely.

"Convinced?" he murmured, running his hands down her body.

"Not yet." She gasped as his mouth latched onto her breast.

Sandy was on fire. And McCade was too. She could tell from the urgency of his mouth, the roughness of his touch, the feverish light in his eyes.

She wrapped her legs around him, pulling him in closer, even closer to her. She could feel his arousal against her—it wouldn't take much effort for him to be inside her.

She lifted her hips, and this time he didn't pull back. He thrust into her, hard and deep, filling her so perfectly, making her feel impossibly complete. He looked down into her eyes and held himself absolutely still, locked together with her. The muscles in his shoulders and arms were tight as he held himself above her.

"I was wondering if we were ever actually going to get around to this," Sandy said breathlessly, "or if we were just going to spend the rest of our lives in foreplay."

"Or talking about fishing." His voice was oddly tight. "You were the one who started the whole conversation about fishing, remember?"

She laughed, and her movement pressed him more deeply inside of her. McCade drew in a sharp breath.

"Sandy, I want to make love to you slowly," he whispered. "I want to savor every second. I want it to last for hours and hours, but baby, you turn me on so much, I think I'm gonna burst—"

His soft words provided the final fuel to the fire that was burning fast and hot inside of her. She pulled his mouth down to hers as she began to move underneath him.

McCade heard himself moan as he matched her every move. He drove himself into her, harder, faster, their pace accelerating with each thrust, sending him dangerously close to the edge. And then he exploded. He could hear his voice as if from a distance, shouting Sandy's name as a cannonball of pleasure ripped through him.

Somehow she followed. He could feel her body racked with the waves of her own release, heard her answering cries of pleasure, saw the rapture on her beautiful face through the haze of his eruption.

He held her tightly until their pounding hearts began to slow.

"I'm convinced," Sandy said, her voice muffled against his shoulder.

He lifted himself off of her on still shaky arms and rolled to the side, pulling her with him. "Convinced?"

"That you love me," she said. She traced his lips lightly with her fingers. "You couldn't have made love to me like that if you didn't."

"I wanted to make love to you all night long." Mc-Cade closed his eyes. "Man, I didn't even last three minutes."

"What, did you time yourself?" she teased. "Come on, McCade, don't tell me you've forgotten your mother's third rule for manly success: 'When it comes to making love, it's not how long you do it that matters, it's how *well* you do it.' And *I* happen to think we did it extremely well."

He opened his eyes. "Her third rule had to do with—"

"Penis size. Right." Sandy rolled her eyes. "I know. I just figured since you've obviously got *that* department handled, I'd give you a variation on the rule."

McCade started to laugh. "Lord, I love you," he said. "You're right. That *was* great, wasn't it?"

"Damn straight. I vote we do it again, real soon." She glanced at him from underneath her eyelashes. "Assuming, of course, that, unlike fishing, it's something you'd want to try again."

"Would you please *stop* with the fishing?"

Her eyes sparkled as she laughed and McCade's heart turned a somersault of joy in his chest. Every day for the rest of his life, he was going to hear her laughter. Every night for the rest of his life, he was going to hold her in his arms like this.

"You know, I came to Phoenix because I'd finally figured out that I was in love with you," he admitted.

Startled, she looked up at him.

"Yeah." He smiled ruefully into her eyes. "I thought I could just ring your doorbell and tell you that I loved you. But it wasn't that easy, and then you blew me away when you told me about James. He sounded so perfect, and I was so scared that I'd lost my chance with you. . . ."

Sandy could barely make sense of his words. Clint had come to Phoenix because he *loved* her? And then, God, she'd gone and hit him over the head with James.

She'd never known McCade to be anything but self-assured and confident. But as she looked into his eyes she saw the reflection of all the things she'd said about wanting James, about her attraction to that man.

"I mean," McCade said quietly, "the guy's already a law partner in a big firm and he's probably going to be lieutenant governor if Harcourt wins the campaign. He's got it made, Sandy. He was born with not just a silver spoon, but a whole damn utensil drawer." He took a deep breath. "James is everything I'm not."

"James?" Sandy met his gaze steadily. "James who?"

McCade's face relaxed into a smile and then he laughed.

"I love *you*, Clint." She smiled. "Need to be convinced?"

He pulled her close and kissed her. "Definitely," he said. "Convince me."

TEN

The shades were pulled down and the room was still dark when the clock radio burst into song. Sandy woke up instantly and lay awake for a moment, mentally reviewing the day's schedule and listening to the cheerful country tune. The music took a little bit longer to penetrate McCade's sleep-soddened brain, and he stirred, then muttered something unintelligible, burrowing down under the covers.

Sandy reached across him to shut off the radio and he grabbed her, pulling the covers over their heads.

"Good morning," he said, his voice thick and raspy with sleep. He kissed her and the stubble on his unshaven face was rough against her cheeks.

She had to get up. She had meetings all morning. But as he kissed her one more time she felt herself melt. She was going to be late—again.

It had been a week since they'd returned from the Grand Canyon. It had been a week full of laughter and lovemaking, a week to learn all about Clint McCade on this new level, a week to get used to waking up to find him in her bed.

But she couldn't get used to any of it. She wasn't sure she ever would. At times it seemed things hadn't changed between them. On the nights that they didn't have to work late, they went out, just as they had before. They had dinner, went down to the billiard hall to shoot some pool, or took in a movie. They laughed and joked and teased each other the way they always had. They were best friends—that hadn't changed. But they were lovers now, too, and Sandy would often turn to find McCade watching her. The look in his eyes would remind her of the love they'd made the night before and his smile would promise more of the same later on, when they were finally alone.

Sandy couldn't remember ever being so happy. She celebrated her happiness noisily, determined to wring every last drop of enjoyment from it. She knew it wasn't going to last forever, and she was so afraid it would end sooner than she hoped.

As she lay in McCade's arms, their passion spent, she refused to think about the future. The question was always there, though, gnawing at her. How long? Just how long did she have before he left?

McCade rode his motorcycle into Scottsdale to shop. The wind had removed every trace of styling from his hair, and as he walked into the little jewelry store, he ran his fingers through it, glancing at his reflection in the mirrored wall. His hair was getting long, and it refused to be tamed. It no longer stayed combed back, instead falling constantly into his eyes.

McCade's eyes narrowed as he looked at himself.

With his worn-out jeans and his dragon tattoo peeking out from under the tight sleeve of his faded black T-shirt, he looked like the old McCade, like a biker from Jersey. He certainly didn't look like an upwardly mobile man who had been attending country-club functions.

He frowned harder at the mirror. Lately he and Sandy had been hanging out in pool halls and road-house-style bars. She hadn't complained, but it was entirely possible that she felt as uncomfortable in those places as he felt standing and chatting in the clubhouse bar next to the ninth hole. He felt a flash of guilt, a stab of uneasiness. Did being with him mean the end of her dream of joining a more sophisticated social world?

Yet she loved him. Sandy honest-to-God loved him. He didn't doubt that. If he did, he wouldn't be in here right now, with the store's owner glaring at him suspiciously. Man, the guy looked as if he couldn't decide whether to take out the gun that was hidden under the counter or call the police.

McCade was more amused than annoyed. "How ya doing?" He smiled at the elderly man, carefully keeping his stance loose and nonaggressive. He crossed to the counter and rested his hands on it, giving the man a silent message: See? No weapons, no threat. "I'm in the market for a ring," he said, and the shop owner relaxed noticeably. "Something with a diamond."

"May I inquire as to the occasion?" the store owner politely asked after clearing his throat.

"Yeah. I'm looking for an engagement ring."

He couldn't keep what he knew was a goofy smile off his face, and the little old man smiled back and led him to another counter.

He saw the ring he wanted to get Sandy immediately.

It was a single diamond, cut traditionally, in a six-prong setting with a plain gold band. "That one." He pointed down at it.

The old man started to look nervous again. "Perhaps we should start by determining your price range, sir," he said so very tactfully.

"Uh-oh. How much?"

It took a great deal of throat clearing before the words emerged. "Three thousand nine hundred and—"

"Can I pay in cash?" McCade interrupted him, "or should I put it on my gold card?"

When Sandy pulled into the carport after work, McCade's bike was gone. It didn't mean anything, she told herself, trying to quell the nervous feelings that were starting to tighten her chest. So his motorcycle was gone, big deal. He'd gone out somewhere, shopping or something. Or . . . out for a ride.

On the highway, maybe? To feel the wind in his hair and the road beneath his wheels? To again taste the freedom he was lacking these days?

She'd stopped at the grocery store on the way home, and now she carried the bags of food up to her apartment, trying not to think. McCade had gone to the store. That's all. She refused to consider the possibility that he'd gotten on Route 10 heading out of town. But of course it *was* possible that he had, and it *was* possible that the pull of the open road had been too strong, and if that was the case, then he was already in New Mexico.

Purposefully calm, she put the key in the lock, turned it, and opened the door. She wouldn't allow herself to rush to the front closet to see if McCade's black leather jacket was still hanging there. She took the groceries into the kitchen, set the bags on the counter, and—

His jacket was hanging on the back of one of the kitchen chairs. He couldn't have gone far. He never would have left without his jacket.

Relief made her dizzy, and with the relief came a wave of anger—anger at herself. McCade might be a wanderer, he might be free and easy with his affections, he might be a lot of things, but he wasn't the kind of man who would leave without saying good-bye.

Sandy put the frozen fruit bars she'd bought into the freezer, then pushed the button on the answering machine and listened to her phone messages as she stored the rest of the groceries.

There was a cheerful message from her mother in Florida, just calling to say hello, thanking her for a birthday present.

Frank had called right after she left the office. He wanted to talk to McCade—something about a major-league baseball trade had him all excited.

The last message on the machine was also for McCade. Sandy was running water into the big pasta pot, starting dinner, but she turned off the faucet to listen.

"Yes, this is Graham Parks from GCH Productions out in Santa Monica. I'm looking for Clint McCade. I need a cameraman for a project that starts in less than two weeks out in Key West, in Florida. It's a documentary we're producing for the Underwater Communications Group about their dolphin language studies. I got your name from Harry Stein at Soundwave Studios, he said you've done some underwater work before and that you're a certified diver. I realize this is very last minute, but the guy I had lined up had an accident, his leg is in traction, and, well . . . The shoot should be completed in three or four weeks. I really hope you're available. Call me ASAP."

Parks left his number and the answering machine beeped twice. There were no other messages.

Sandy stood at the sink, staring sightlessly at the pot of water she still held.

This project started in less than two weeks.

Less than two weeks.

It couldn't have been a more enticing offer. Clint had done a number of underwater shoots before, and they were among his very favorites.

Sandy turned to look at the answering machine, tempted to push the erase button, to make the message disappear. But she couldn't. She couldn't do it to Mc-Cade, and she couldn't do it to herself—if she did, she'd always believe he'd stayed with her because he didn't know there was a better offer in Florida. No, she couldn't make the message disappear. She had to play it for him.

And then *McCade* would disappear.

McCade could smell the spaghetti sauce cooking as he came into the condo. Sandy was in the kitchen, making a salad. She glanced up at him. "Hey. You're back."

She'd changed out of her work clothes and was wearing cutoffs and a halter top. He came up behind her and pushed her hair off her shoulders.

"Hey?" He kissed her lightly on the neck. "That's all the greeting I get today?"

She turned and stood on her toes to kiss him. He pulled her in close and didn't release her, deepening the kiss until he felt her relax against him. "That's much better," he said as he smiled into her eyes.

"Where'd you go?"

McCade hesitated, not wanting to tell her he'd been to the jewelers. "Oh, you know," he told her vaguely. "Just out."

Sandy pulled free from his arms, turning her attention to the salad. "Riding around?" she asked with her back to him.

"Yeah." He gladly grabbed that as an alibi. It wasn't as if he was really lying. He *did* ride his motorcycle to and from the store.

"Oh."

McCade lifted the lid on the pot that held the sauce. Man, it smelled great. He reached around her to wash his hands in the sink. Sandy had already put several woven place mats on the kitchen table, and he fished in the silverware drawer for forks and knives, and set them on the table along with two napkins.

"There're a couple of messages for you on the machine," Sandy told him, still focused on the salad. "The last two."

She heard him cross to the answering machine as she concentrated on cutting up a cucumber. He'd been out riding his bike, with no destination in mind, the way he did when he was feeling restless. After McCade heard the message from that Graham Parks guy, he was as good as gone.

The tape chirped as he rewound it.

The message from Frank played, then came the job offer.

Sandy didn't turn around, but she heard McCade become very, very still as he listened. And then she heard the sound of a pen on paper as he wrote down the phone number. She waited for him to speak, but he didn't. He was looking at her—she could feel his eyes, even though her back was turned.

"You can return his call in the bedroom if you want." To her relief her voice came out level and calm.

"Sandy."

She turned around slowly. McCade was standing near the counter that held the answering machine, the piece of paper with Graham Parks's phone number in one hand. He used the other hand to push his hair back from his face.

She couldn't look at him without wanting to touch him, to run her own fingers through his sun-streaked hair, to wrap herself around him, to hold on tight and never let go—

"You could come too." His eyes looked turquoise in the early-evening light that filtered through the kitchen window. "Key West is beautiful," he said. "You'd love it there. We could make it a . . . a vacation. We could even take a couple of days on one end and visit your mother."

"There's no way I can take three or four weeks off." Sandy turned, busily wiping her hands on the towel looped around the refrigerator-door handle.

"Sure, you could," he argued. "Frank's chomping at the bit, dying to do some producing of his own. Leave him in charge, he'll do a great job—"

"It wouldn't be a vacation—you'd be working."

"You could assist me. Or better yet, have your own camera. We could swim with dolphins, Sand. It would be so great. Let me talk to Parks—"

"I've never gone scuba diving." Sandy didn't want to be having this conversation. "I'm not qualified. I never even really learned to swim—you know that. I can't do more than a doggy paddle. It wouldn't work."

"Yes, it would—"

"No, Clint. It wouldn't."

"Aw, come on. *Dolphins*, Sandy—"

"You're a big boy, McCade," she said sharply. "You don't need me to go along. Just call up Parks and tell him you'll take the job."

The timer buzzed angrily, and Sandy reached across the stove to turn it off.

McCade watched her drain the bubbling pot of pasta into the colander in the sink. "I may not need you to come along," he finally said, "but I want you to."

Sandy felt tears sting her eyelids. Oh, God, she thought, don't let me cry. "Maybe I could take a week . . ." But then what? Then she'd have to get back on a plane, all alone, and fly back to Phoenix, all alone. And wait, all alone, wondering if McCade was going to return, or if he was going to find some new, incredibly fascinating project to work on. Three or four weeks could quickly turn into three or four months. If she was lucky, she'd see him again next December.

"One week's not long enough." There was no way he was going to take a job that separated him from Sandy for two or three whole weeks. Not now. Maybe in a year, when their relationship was more solid. But for right now, as much as he wanted to swim with the dolphins down on Key West, he wanted to be with Sandy more.

He picked up the telephone and punched in the number Parks had left. Graham Parks picked up.

"Clint McCade! Great! Thanks for returning my call so quickly." His voice boomed over the line. "I realized after I left the message I didn't give you the exact dates. We start shooting on the twentieth of May, but U. Comm wants the underwater team to come down to their facilities by May fifteenth at the latest. Apparently, there's certain dolphin etiquette involved. They feel it would be invasive to the dolphins if our cameramen simply showed up one day and jumped into the tank without any of what they call 'courtship' time."

"Sounds fair to me. I wouldn't want strangers jumping into *my* tank unintroduced."

"Harry Stein said you're the best when it comes to underwater photography," Parks said. "What the hell are you doing in the middle of the desert? No, don't answer that. Just tell me you'll sign on."

"I'm afraid I can't. I'm sorry, I—"

Sandy snatched the phone from him. "Excuse me, Mr. Parks, can you hold on for just one moment, please?" she said very sweetly into the telephone. Then she glared at McCade, cupping the receiver with her hand so Parks couldn't hear their conversation. "Are you nuts? You can't turn down this job."

"Yes, I can—"

"But I *know* you want to do it!" She shook her head. "Shoot, McCade, if you don't take it, you'll wish you had, and then you'll blame me!"

"I will *not!*" He sounded insulted. "God, Kirk, I'm not a child. I can make a decision without—"

Sandy moved her hand from the telephone receiver to cover his mouth. "Mr. Parks?" she said. "When do you need McCade's final decision?"

"Now," he said, but then laughed. "Except if it's no, which it sure sounded like it was going to be. Is there any chance at all that he'll change his mind?"

"No," McCade mumbled from underneath Sandy's hand.

"Yes," she said.

"Then he can have till Saturday," Parks told her.

"But if he comes to a decision earlier, I'd appreciate being informed."

Sandy hung up the phone and turned toward Mc-Cade. He was standing with his arms crossed and a very keen glint of displeasure in his eyes.

"*Damm*it," he fumed. "The man needs to know so he can start trying to find another cameraman. You of all people should know how even a few extra days can make a difference to a producer in a bind—"

"I want you to take the job."

Some of the anger in his eyes turned to bewilderment. "Why?"

She turned away, unable to look at him. "Get real, McCade. You don't honestly expect me to believe that you're going to live here with me, happily ever after, and never take another job out of state again, do you?"

"Of course not," he countered hotly. "We both know that would never work. But I'm just not ready to leave yet."

She gripped the edge of the kitchen counter. He'd admitted it. He'd finally admitted that he wasn't going to stick around forever. "What difference does it make," she asked tightly, "whether you leave now or later?"

Either way, he was going to leave. If he waited, if he didn't take this job, he *would* regret it. And she didn't want him to regret anything, not one single thing about their time together.

"It *does* make a difference," he said wildly. "It makes an enormous difference." He took her arm, but she pulled away. "Dammit, don't hide from me!"

Sandy lifted her gaze to his defiantly, and she knew he could see the tears that filled her eyes.

He swore. "I love you, dammit." He gripped her shoulders, holding her chin up so that she had to keep looking at him. "I said I didn't need you to come with me, but I was lying. I *do* need you. I *need* you."

McCade kissed her fiercely, almost frantically, invading her senses with his taste, his scent, his touch.

"I need you," he whispered again, "all the time. I need you next to me at night. I need you there to talk to. I need to see your face, to see you smile at me. I need to make love to you—"

Sandy wasn't sure whether to laugh or cry, so she did a little of both as she kissed him.

She heard McCade groan as her hands slid down into the back pockets of his jeans, as she pressed her body against his. He returned her kisses as he deftly unfastened her halter top, as his fingers searched for the button on her shorts. Her clothes fell to the floor.

With one sweep of his arm, he cleared off the kitchen table, the silverware clattering as it hit the ground. He lifted her up so she was sitting on its surface, and as she pulled off his T-shirt he unfastened his pants and then, Lord, he was inside of her. She clung to him, her legs locked around his waist, pulling him into her, driving him deeper, harder, faster.

Sandy pulled McCade down on top of her as she leaned back against the table, thrilling at the way he filled her, at the way he made her feel. She loved it when he lost control, and this time he was wild, possessed by a storm of passion that carried her with him to new heights. Her heart pounded with a primitive rhythm, a rhythm that speeded up with each thrust of McCade's body. Fire surged through her veins, a fire she knew was destined to burn for all her life. She loved McCade, deeply, passionately—and unendingly.

Sandy opened her eyes and looked up at the expression of sheer pleasure that was on his face. As if he could feel her watching him, his eyes opened and he smiled at her. It was that smile, that quick, fierce, familiar grin that sent her spinning, spiraling into ecstasy, with wave upon wave of pleasure soaring through her, causing her body to shake. She felt McCade's release, a white-hot explosion that left him out of breath and spent, lying across her.

"Mercy," he murmured, shifting his weight.

Sandy was laughing. "I can't believe we just did it on the kitchen table," she said. "I'm not going to be able to eat a meal here again without thinking about tonight. Unless I get a new table, I'm going to remember this forever—at least twice a day, during breakfast and dinner."

"Good." McCade couldn't keep the satisfaction from his voice. "Then you'll also remember at least twice a day how much I love you."

Sandy kissed him, strangely saddened by his words. She should feel happy—he loved her.

She'd never forget that.

But someday he would.

Tony looked at McCade critically in the mirror, then took another fraction of an inch off the sides of his hair.

"So tell me, sweetheart, why is it *really* that you don't want to take this job in Florida?" the heavyset hairdresser asked, raising one thick, dark eyebrow.

"I told you," McCade said. "I don't want to go. Sandy's just getting used to me being around, and I don't want the job. Really."

"If you didn't want the job"—Tony crossed his arms—"you never would have mentioned it to me."

"I was making conversation."

"I don't think so, McCade."

McCade laughed. "Right. You're so smart, Tony, *you* tell me why I don't want to go to Florida."

"Because you know if you leave now, Sandy will think you're leaving for good." Tony's eyes were nearly hidden by folds of flesh as he smiled smugly at McCade's reflection in the mirror.

McCade swore under his breath. He hated to admit it, but Tony was right. That was definitely part of the reason he didn't want to go. He'd seen the sadness lurking in Sandy's eyes. No matter what he told her, no matter what he said, she didn't believe he was really going to stick around. He hoped after tonight that was going to change.

"You want some advice?" Tony asked.

"No."

"The only way she's ever going to think you're really going to stay is if you leave." He held up a mirror so that McCade could see the back of his head. "It's a paradox. She'll think you're gone for good, but when you come back, she'll know she was wrong."

"Terrific," McCade growled, rolling his eyes. "I'm supposed to give Parks my answer by today. That fits in really nicely with my plan to ask Sandy to marry me tonight."

Tony stared. "Did you just say . . . ?" He laughed, dancing in a circle around McCade's chair. "I knew it, I knew it," he singsonged. "Oh, this is *too* good. Clint McCade *married*."

"Knock it off," McCade said crossly, standing up.

Tony stopped dancing and smiled at his friend, his brown eyes warm. "Sandy's going to be one happy lady tonight." He shook McCade's hand in congratulations. "Tonight, and the rest of her life."

McCade smiled, but he wondered—not for the first time—if he was doing the right thing. He knew it would be more than right for him. But for Sandy? He headed for the door, unable to shake the feeling that he was getting away with something here.

ELEVEN

The collar of McCade's tuxedo shirt was way too tight. He stood, sipping his soda, watching Sandy work her way around the room at Simon Harcourt's side.

The Harcourt project had come full circle, and they were back at the Pointe resort for the first public screening of the thirty-minute mini-documentary Video Enterprises had put together for the Harcourt campaign.

It had been good. Very good. It was classily done and extremely effective.

McCade moved slightly to the side so he could see her. She was wearing her favorite dress, the black slip dress with the string straps. Her hair was piled high on her head, a few stray locks falling down around her smooth shoulders. She looked charming and sexy. She also looked elegant, beautiful, calm, and in control.

The man she was talking to stepped aside, and McCade realized James Vandenberg was there, too, standing at Harcourt's other shoulder. Sandy's attention was on the man in front of her, but Vandenberg was watching her. McCade's fingers tightened on his glass as he saw Vandenberg's eyes start a slow amble south from Sandy's face.

Relax, McCade ordered himself. The woman was a knockout. Men were going to look at her. And that's all Vandenberg was doing, just looking.

He could feel the weight of the jewelry box in the inside pocket of his tuxedo jacket. A few hours from now, when this party was over, he'd take Sandy aside and . . . McCade smiled. After she had his ring on her finger, James would certainly think twice about giving her the eye.

"Clint McCade, isn't it?" A voice at his shoulder made him turn around. "I'm very good with names."

It was portly, florid Aaron Fields, the guy from Channel Five, the guy Sandy had dated once, with such disastrous results that she *still* hadn't told McCade the whole story. Standing next to Fields was a thin long-nosed man who seemed very bored.

Fields held out his hand and said, "Aaron Fields, Channel Five." He pointed to his companion. "This is Jim Grove, assistant producer."

"How ya doin'?" McCade switched his glass of soda to his left hand in order to shake.

"I was glad we found that footage of Harcourt in our archives," Fields said. "You know, the film from that community center? That was ours."

McCade nodded. "I thought Sandy—*Cassandra* used that piece well."

"Yeah." Fields looked over McCade's shoulder, obviously not listening.

The thin man was also looking at something behind McCade, so he followed their gaze across the room to where Sandy was shaking the hand of an elderly woman.

Fields motioned with the hand holding his drink for Grove's benefit.

"That's Cassandra, the killer blonde in the little black number." He turned to McCade. "I heard through the grapevine that she's seeing you these days."

McCade made himself smile pleasantly. "That's right."

"You're happy about that, huh?" Fields smirked back. "I bet. When I first heard you two were an item, it really bothered me—you're the *cameraman*, for chrissake. You'd think she'd go for a director or a producer, someone who's *somebody*, someone with clout instead of some lowly techie. I was actually surprised she didn't hook up with James Vandenberg. Now, *there's* a man with power. . . ." He shook his head, looking back across the room at Sandy and James.

McCade tried to quell the anger that was building in him. This guy was an idiot, a fool, a jerk. Nothing he said should be taken seriously. Still, he turned to the smaller man, freezing him with a black look and a dangerous smile. "Lucky this lowly techie is so easygoing, or he might take that as an insult," he said.

"Hey, no offense, I just figured . . ." Fields shrugged and turned to Grove.

McCade began to move away, but he stopped when he heard Fields say, "I don't know what the big deal is. Turns out Mr. McCade's an Emmy Award–winning cameraman. 'Course, Video Enterprises couldn't possibly have the kind of budget they'd need to pay him what he's worth, so Cassandra Kirk puts out to get what she wants. She did the same thing with me when I had that tape she wanted and—"

"You *lying* son of a bitch!"

McCade reached for Fields's shoulder and swung

him around . . . knowing he shouldn't. Part of him stood helplessly by and watched as the rest of him hauled back and popped Aaron Fields in the nose.

He noted with some detachment that Fields actually rose slightly off the ground, landing somewhat gracelessly and bowling over a passing waiter who was carrying a tray of champagne glasses.

Guests within a twenty-foot radius were showered with the wine. There were screams and squeals of surprise that turned to cries of outrage as Aaron Fields hauled himself to his feet, blood pouring from his nose.

McCade had to hand it to the guy. He didn't have much in the way of brains, but he knew enough not to launch himself at McCade and continue what surely would have been a losing battle. Instead, Fields drew himself up to his full height. "You'll be hearing from my lawyer."

"Fine," McCade said. "When you call him, you might mention the words 'defamation of character.' "

Fields was undaunted. "The words 'assault and battery' come more readily to mind."

McCade laughed. "Battery? I don't think so." He took a threatening step toward Fields, who instantly cowered. "You want battery? Step outside, and I'll batter your butt across the parking lot, scumbag."

"What's going on here?" It was James Vandenberg, cool, calm, and collected. The crowd parted for him, and he stepped between the two men.

"This man assaulted me." Fields again pointed accusingly at McCade.

Sandy pushed through the crowd, and McCade saw the look of shock on her face, the flare of anger in her eyes.

As McCade watched she pulled Vandenberg aside

and spoke softly into his ear. The lawyer nodded, and Sandy disappeared back into the crowd, without a second glance at McCade.

James took both Fields and McCade firmly by the arm. "Gentlemen, perhaps we could continue this conversation outside . . . ?"

The night air felt hot after the air-conditioned lobby. Once they were out on the driveway, away from the staring eyes of Harcourt's guests, James crossed his arms. "What the *hell* is going on here?"

"I want to call the police." Fields held his bloodied handkerchief to his nose. "I want to press charges."

"Did you hit him?" James asked McCade.

"Yeah, I did," McCade said evenly. "He said some things about Sandy and—"

"I think my nose is broken," whined Fields.

"If your nose was broken," McCade told him, "you wouldn't just think it. You'd *know* it. Trust me. Besides, I didn't hit you hard enough to break it."

Fields began to sputter again, and James pulled him aside. The lawyer's voice was too low for McCade to hear, so he leaned against a pole that supported the awning at the entrance of the resort and waited, wishing he still smoked, wishing he had a cigarette.

Sandy had been pretty damn mad. And the way she'd walked away without even looking at him . . . *That* had really stung. He wanted to go back inside, to find her and try to explain what had happened, what Fields had said about her. He stood up and moved toward the door, but Vandenberg glanced up at him, giving him a "don't move" look. The guy would've made a great high-school principal.

He wasn't sure just what Vandenberg said to Fields, but the end result was that Fields was escorted to the nearby medical center in a sleek, white limousine, with one of Harcourt's aides dancing attendance.

As the taillights of the car disappeared down the driveway, Vandenberg turned coolly to McCade. "I'm going to have to ask you to leave," he said. "Why don't you take Cassandra's car? I'll give her a lift home."

McCade laughed, but there was no humor in it. "Yeah, right. Not a chance, Vandenberg."

"Have we had a little too much to drink tonight? Should I call you a cab?"

"*We* have been drinking nothing but cola all evening long." He crossed his arms. "I'll wait out here for Sandy. Cassandra. Thank you very much."

"I'm afraid that's not possible. I'd like you to leave the resort property."

McCade took a deep breath, calming himself down. "Look, the guy was being a jerk."

"And what were *you*, McCade?" James countered sternly. "Cassandra's in there, talking to a representative from the Arizona Board of Tourism, trying to negotiate a deal to do some of the state's travel commercials. And what do *you* do? You start a *brawl*! What's she supposed to say? 'Excuse me while I go see if my date—who also happens to be one of my employees—has broken some poor slob's nose?' "

"I didn't know." McCade swore softly, squeezing his eyes shut. "I didn't think—"

"No kidding. Why don't you do both Cassandra and Mr. Harcourt a favor and make yourself scarce? All we need is a little media involvement to turn this into a real three-ring circus."

McCade turned to walk away, down the driveway, but then turned back. "I'm sorry," he said quietly, sincerely.

"Go back to California, McCade." Vandenberg was unmoved by the apology. "Cassandra will be better off without you. You're not good enough for her."

McCade bit back the words he wanted to say, the words that would tell James Vandenberg quite explicitly and concisely what to do with himself. The lawyer expected him to say them, was waiting for him to do so, a small smile playing about his perfect mouth. But McCade was damned if he'd give the other man that satisfaction.

Silently, he turned and walked away, down the driveway, into the darkness of the hot Arizona night.

McCade was sitting on the back of his motorcycle, waiting for Sandy as she pulled into the carport.

He got to his feet as she climbed out of the driver's seat and she stared at him unsmilingly.

The silence was deafening, and McCade moistened his lips nervously. Damn, she was furious with him.

What could he say? "I'm sorry."

She laughed, but it was more like a sob. "And that's supposed to make it all better?"

"I don't know what else to say," McCade told her quietly. "I can't tell you that I wouldn't do it over again exactly the same way, because I probably would. The guy deserved it—"

It was obvious that Sandy had been on a slow burn for the past two hours, and now she all but exploded. "What about me, McCade? Did *I* deserve it? *How* could you do that to me?" she asked, her voice rising. "How could you start a fight at the most important event of my career? God, I was *mortified!*"

"I said I was sorry—"

"You're sorry. That's just great. You're sorry." Sandy slammed the car door shut. "I've worked *hard* to get where I am in life, and you come damned close to ruining all of that in one single night with your stupid, no-brain, low-class behavior!" She started pacing, unable to contain her anger, unable to stand still. "I left all that back in New Jersey, back in that crummy apartment complex with the bugs and the rats and the neighbors who shouted and threw things at each other all night long. I got out of there, McCade, and where I went, people don't just haul off and hit other people—in the *nose*, of all places—in the middle of a party!"

McCade stood quietly. She was right. She had every reason to be angry with him.

"You were lucky Aaron Fields didn't demand to press charges!" she continued. "That would've looked great in the paper in the morning. 'Video Producer's Lover Hauled Off to Jail!' "

"Don't you even want to know why I hit him?"

"No!" Sandy shouted, then worked to lower her voice. "No, I don't! *Why* you hit him is irrelevant. The fact is, there's no place for violence of *any* kind, for *any* reason, at a place like the Pointe. It's not a biker bar, McCade! Fighting isn't an acceptable form of communication among *my* friends and business associates! If you can't learn that, then maybe you should just go to Florida! Maybe you'll have better luck communicating with the dolphins!"

As soon as the words were out of her mouth, she wished she could take them back. McCade looked dazed.

"You're right, I don't fit in. I can't change any more than I already have, and still there's no place for me in your world. You should have left me behind with the rats and the roaches." He looked at her, pain in his eyes. "Or maybe you already have," he whispered, "and I just haven't noticed."

With a jump, he kick-started the Harley.

"Clint, wait!" Sandy shouted, but he didn't hear her over the roar of his bike. She ran toward him, but before she could reach him, he'd peeled out, leaving behind the stench of burning rubber and the echo of her harsh, angry words.

It was after three o'clock in the morning before McCade returned. Sandy was waiting up for him on the couch. She stood up as he came into the apartment.

"I'm sorry," she told him. "I didn't mean what I said, Clint."

McCade looked at her. The words stuck in his throat, but he had to say them. He'd made up his mind, and now he had to follow through. "I think it's probably time for me to go."

His eyes filled with fresh tears, and he swallowed hard, blinking them back. Dammit, he couldn't let her see him cry.

"No—"

He had to look away. She wasn't hiding her own tears, and the sight of her crying was too much.

He had to get out of there. Fast.

"James Vandenberg was right," he murmured. Sandy *would* be better off without him. "I called Graham Parks and told him I'd take the Florida job. You were right all along," he lied. "I really want that job. And it's probably time for me to move on."

Sandy stared at him in silence, and McCade felt sick, seeing the pain his words had caused. But if he stuck around, he'd hurt her far more in the long run. He had to hold on to that thought.

She nodded, and her quiet acceptance made him ache. She'd expected him to leave. Despite all of his words of love and promises of forever, she hadn't believed him. And now here he was, forced to prove her right.

"When?" she asked softly.

"I think it would be better if I went tonight."

McCade went into the bedroom and quickly changed out of his tuxedo. He hung it neatly in Sandy's closet, next to the pants and shirts she'd bought him. Where he was going he wouldn't need a tuxedo, and he didn't want to wear those other clothes.

He slipped on his jeans and a clean T-shirt. His other pair of jeans went into his duffel bag, along with the rest of his T-shirts and his underwear. He tried not to think as he packed, tried not to feel.

He carried the duffel bag to the entry hall and took his leather jacket from the closet, setting it all down by the front door. His camera case was in the living room, and he went to get it, checking to make sure the latches were locked.

"Stay for tonight, Clint." Sandy's voice was so soft, he almost couldn't make out her words. Almost.

She was sitting on the couch, her face pale, her eyes big and full of hurt. McCade had to look away.

He wanted to stay. Lord, how he wanted to stay. But he wanted to stay for forever, not just for tonight. There was no way he could sleep in her bed tonight, no way he could make love to her without giving himself away.

And he wasn't going to do that.

"I don't think that's a good idea."

It was obviously the answer she'd been expecting.

"I gotta go." Hefting his camera in one hand and his duffel bag and jacket in the other, he went out the door, closing it tightly behind him.

Sandy didn't go in to work for four solid days.

She scrubbed her condo until it was clean enough to eat off of the floors. She watched soap operas and reread her favorite books. She slept late and napped in the afternoon. She alphabetized her bookshelves, but didn't like the way it looked, so she reshelved the books according to size and color. She watched her entire video library of romantic comedies, but didn't laugh once.

McCade was gone.

On Thursday, she had a meeting with Simon Harcourt and James Vandenberg that could not be rescheduled. After so many days of wearing nothing but pajamas or baggy shorts, she dressed carefully in her blue-flowered sundress and took extra time with her makeup. She wore her hair down, the way McCade liked it.

It was strange leaving her condo, after four days of isolation. The sun was molten and the air felt like a furnace, hot and dry in her lungs. But it was only late spring. Summer was coming and it was going to be hell.

McCade had the right idea, Sandy thought as she cranked the AC in her car to high. It made sense to travel around the country, moving with the weather. Nothing beat Arizona in January, but July was a different story.

As she drove to work she wondered where McCade would go after he finished filming on Key West. She wondered for the five millionth time since he'd left if she'd ever see him again.

She'd toyed with the idea of buying a plane ticket to

Miami and following him. What would he do if she just suddenly showed up in Florida? God, what if he'd already found another lover? But even if he hadn't, nothing would be different, nothing would have changed. All she would have done was buy a little more time, put off the inevitable—because the sad truth was, McCade had finally admitted that he loved his freedom more than he loved her.

She pulled into the Video Enterprises parking lot.

McCade was gone. She was simply going to have to get used to that. McCade was gone, and chasing after him wasn't going to bring him back.

According to the schedule, Frank Williamson was in studio A, shooting part of a music video. The red "in progress" light above the studio entrance was not on, and Sandy pushed the door open. The members of the band stood talking to Frank in front of a blue screen. The rest of the studio was dark. A camera was positioned near her in the shadows. She stepped inside.

"Gary, would you tell Frank I want to—"

It wasn't Gary standing behind the camera. It wasn't O'Reilly either.

It was McCade.

Shocked, Sandy stared directly into his eyes for a good five seconds before he looked away.

"What are you doing here?" she whispered, hardly daring to breathe, hardly daring to hope.

"I promised Frank I'd help him out with this video." He wouldn't meet her eyes. "I don't have to be in Key West for another four days, so . . ." He shrugged.

He obviously wasn't there to see her.

She nodded, fighting the disappointment. "Will you please tell Frank I'd like to talk to him when he gets a chance." Somehow she managed to keep her voice level.

"Sure." He glanced into her eyes for maybe half a second before looking away again. But then he looked back. "You okay?" he asked softly.

Looking into his eyes was like being sucked into a whirlpool. Sandy realized at that moment that she was never going to recover. She was going to love this man for the rest of her life, whether he loved her back or not. She turned away before he could see her sudden tears.

No, she was not okay. She would never be okay again.

"I'm fine."

McCade watched her close the door gently behind her. She looked good, a little tired maybe, but good. She said she was fine; hell, she was probably half over him already.

That was good, that was what he wanted, right?

So how come it made him feel so bad?

TWELVE

The telephone was ringing as Sandy unlocked the door. Once inside the condo, she threw down her briefcase and ran for the kitchen. As she picked up the phone the answering machine clicked on, and she shouted to be heard over the recorded message as she struggled to turn the damned thing off.

"Whew!" she said triumphantly, finally. "Sorry. I'm here. You caught me walking in the door."

"That was pretty intense, sweetheart. And you're supposed to be some sort of technical genius or something? At least that's what McCade said. Sure coulda fooled me."

The voice was familiar, but she couldn't quite place it. Was it . . . "Tony?"

"Bingo," the hairdresser answered happily. "Good ear, pumpkin. Is McCade around?"

"Um. No, actually he's not."

"That's okay," Tony said. "I really wanted to talk to you, anyway. When's the happy day?"

Sandy leaned against the kitchen table as she kicked off her shoes. God, her feet hurt. "The what?"

"The happy day," he repeated. "You know, the big event . . . Here comes the bride. All dressed in white . . ." He sang loudly and very off-key. "Is it going to be a big wedding or a small one? Have you picked out your china pattern yet? Did McCade talk you into going to Key West with him for the honeymoon? Come on, sister, tell me. This inquiring mind needs to know."

She sat down heavily in the nearest chair. "Tony, did someone tell you that McCade and I were going to get married?" she asked carefully.

"Someone sure did, dollface." He wheezed slightly as he laughed. "I heard it straight from the horse's mouth."

"That's one hell of a rumor." She fought back the tears that were, again, threatening. "Which horse exactly did you hear it from? I assume you're not talking about Mr. Ed."

"The expression 'the horse's mouth' implies I heard it from the guy who oughta know," Tony said. "You know, *McCade.*"

Sandy hung on to the arms of her chair to keep from falling over. "Tony, McCade moved out Saturday night."

"He did?" His voice rose up a full octave. "But—"

"What did he tell you?" she asked. "Was it something about a guy named Frank and an office bet? Because that was just a joke."

Silence. She could almost hear him thinking.

"Noooo," Tony finally said. "McCade was in here on Saturday afternoon for a haircut. He told me he was planning to stop at the jewelers on his way home. The ring was sized and ready to be picked up. From what he told me, I figured he planned to pop the question that night."

Saturday night. The night McCade had punched Aaron Fields in the nose. The night she had lost her temper and yelled at him, accusing him of God only knows what.

She closed her eyes. "Well, he didn't ask me anything. We had a fight and now he's gone."

Tony swore. "I tell you, that man can be a real fool."

"Are you sure you heard him right?"

"Ain't nothing wrong with my ears, sweetcakes. I remember, I told him he should take the job in Florida, because it was the only way *you'd* ever believe he was going to stick around."

Sandy shook her head. "You lost me there. Leaving doesn't seem to be a very good way to prove that you won't leave."

"Snap to it, Einstein!" Tony barked. "You'd know he was going to stick around when he *came back*, get it? Anyway, after I said that, he said he wasn't going to go to Florida because he was going to ask you to marry him. Or something like that. He *did* use the word 'marry.' " He pronounced it very slowly. "As in get hitched. As in happily ever after?"

It didn't make sense. McCade had claimed he was leaving because it was time to move on, because he wanted to take that Florida job. Yet that very day he'd told Tony he was going to ask Sandy to marry him, and *not* take the job? What was going on?

"Oops, a customer just walked in. I've gotta go. Call me if you need me for *any*thing, all right, honey?"

Sandy thanked him and slowly hung up the phone.

Marriage. *Marriage?*

She stood up and went into her bedroom. She

opened the closet door and stared at the clothes McCade had left behind. He had been wearing his tuxedo that night. What if . . . ?

She took the suit out of the closet, unable to resist holding it up to her face to inhale his familiar scent. Oh, God, she missed him.

Fighting the tears yet again, she went through the pockets. There was nothing in the pants. His black bow tie was neatly folded in one of the outside jacket pockets. The other held a matchbook from the Pointe. But inside the jacket—

There was something. . . .

Sandy reached in and pulled out a jeweler's ring box.

It was small and dark blue velvet, with rounded edges.

She held it in her hands, still refusing to believe that there could be a diamond ring inside of it. It couldn't be—

But it was.

The diamond was huge and elegant in its simple setting. It glittered, reflecting the light with all of its planes and edges. Sandy carefully slipped the ring out of the box. The inner band was engraved with the letters C.M. & S.K., simple and sweet, like lovers' initials carved on a tree.

It *was* an engagement ring, and he'd gotten it for her.

So what the hell had happened to make him change his mind?

She'd shouted at him, that's what had happened. She'd said some awful, unforgivable things. But he'd been no prince that night either. Punching Aaron Fields in the nose . . .

They'd both behaved badly. But was that a reason to

do a complete one-eighty? He'd bought this ring. He must've thought long and hard about marriage.

What else had happened that night?

Sandy closed her eyes, trying to see that night from McCade's point of view.

Fields had obviously provoked him. After he punched Fields out, James had escorted him outside and virtually kicked him out of the party, and—

James.

Right before McCade left for good, he'd said something about James. He'd said that James had been right or something like that. Sandy hadn't understood, and Clint hadn't explained, and the time wasn't right to press the issue.

All right, what else?

McCade had walked home and waited for her in the carport. She got home and—God, she'd been so angry with him! She'd told him to go to Florida, of all the stupid things she could have said! But later she'd apologized and told him that she hadn't meant it.

Of course there was always the possibility that Mc-Cade had simply gotten cold feet. Marriage meant settling down, not disappearing into the Brazilian jungle or the Alaskan tundra for four months at a time. Four weeks, sure, but not four months.

Sandy slipped the ring onto her finger. The fit was perfect.

Why had he changed his mind?

She had to know.

She reached for the telephone. She didn't have to look up Frank's number, it was on her automatic dialing. She keyed in the code and waited for the phone to ring.

Frank picked it up right away. " 'Lo?"

"Frank, it's Sandy," she said. "I need to find Mc-Cade. Do you know where he's staying?"

"Yeah," Frank replied. "He's staying with me. Or he was. Boy, am I glad you finally called, boss. I don't know what you guys fought about, but I've never seen a guy more down. The man is seriously depressed. I was going to call you, but he told me if I as much as breathed a word to you about it, he'd rip out my lungs."

"Is he there?" she asked breathlessly. Was it possible that Clint was as upset about their breakup as she was? Was it possible that he still loved her?

"No. He's freelancing tonight for Channel Eight news. He's with the news team covering the mayor's birthday party downtown. They'll be shooting live from the mayor's house for the ten o'clock news report. But he's not coming back here afterward."

"Why not?" Sandy asked.

"He's leaving for Florida."

"Tonight?"

"His bike's all packed," Frank told her. "He's leaving directly from the mayor's."

"Oh, no." Sandy looked at the clock on her bedside table. Eight twenty-eight. It was eight twenty-eight, and McCade could be on the highway anytime after ten. "Frank, if he calls you, tell him that if he leaves before he talks to me, I'll . . . I'll . . ."

"Rip *his* lungs out?" Frank suggested helpfully.

"Just tell him not to go anywhere."

She hung up and scrambled around looking for her briefcase. She found it in the entryway, and she quickly pulled out her date book, flipping to the list of phone numbers in the back. She got the cordless phone from the kitchen and dialed James Vandenberg's home phone number as she walked back down the hall to her bedroom. Please let him be home, she prayed.

"Hello?"

"James, it's Sandy," she said. "Kirk. Sandy Kirk. I need to get into the mayor's birthday party, and I figured if anyone could think of a way I could sneak in, it would be you."

James laughed. "I'm flattered, I think. And yes, I can think of a way, and you wouldn't be sneaking in. I have an invitation somewhere on my desk. . . ."

She could hear the rustling of papers. Then: "Here it is. You know, the party's already started."

"I don't care." Sandy flipped through the clothes in her closet. What did people wear to a mayoral birthday party? "I need to get in there. McCade's there, and I need to talk to him before he leaves at ten. Can I swing by and pick up the invitation?"

"It's not going to get you into the party unless I'm with you," James told her. "Security's pretty tight and the invitation's in my name. No one's going to mistake *you* for James Vandenberg." He laughed. "You're just not tall enough. Among other things."

Sandy swore.

"This is really that urgent?"

"Yes."

James was silent for a moment. "Funny, I heard through the grapevine that McCade was leaving town."

"He is." She grimly pulled out the white dress McCade had bought her. It had been his very favorite. "But he's not leaving tonight—not if *I* can help it."

"You once told me you knew he was going to leave sooner or later. You said it was inevitable."

"I love him," she said quietly, "and dammit, I'm not going to let him go without a fight."

Another long silence. Then: "All right. How about I change my clothes and pick you up in about twenty-five minutes? Can you be ready?"

"Are you serious?" Sandy wasn't sure she heard him correctly.

"Meet me outside," he told her. "It'll save time."

"Thank you for doing this." Sandy looked over at James. His face was lit by the soft glow of light from the dashboard of his Jaguar.

He smiled. "You look beautiful."

"Thanks." Sandy glanced down at her left hand. She was wearing the ring McCade had bought for her. He may not have asked the question, but she was giving him an answer anyway. Yes, she would marry him. Now, if only they got there in time . . .

"You sure McCade is worth all of this effort?"

"Absolutely."

"You really love him that much?"

"If he leaves, I don't know what I'm going to do." She was silent for a moment, then added, "Yeah, I *do* know what I'm going to do. I'm going to be miserable forever."

James slowed the Jaguar to make a right turn. "I guess I was wrong."

"About what?" she asked, checking her watch. It was closing in on ten o'clock. Had it been a light news day? If it had been a light news day, Channel 8 would most likely use the mayor's party as a lead story. They'd spend two, maybe three minutes on it at the most. . . .

"I really thought that you'd be better off without McCade."

Sandy stared at him.

"But I was wrong, wasn't I?" he said.

"You didn't—" She took a deep breath and started again. "You didn't, by any chance, tell McCade that, did you?"

He had the decency to look embarrassed. "Well, yes. I guess I probably did."

"Saturday night?" she asked, even though she knew the answer.

"Yeah," James admitted. "It was after his fight with Aaron Fields. I also told him . . ." He grimaced, not wanting to say the words.

"What?"

"That he wasn't good enough for you. I'm sorry. I shouldn't have interfered."

"Damn right you shouldn't have!" Sandy squeezed her eyes shut, remembering her own words to McCade. What had she said—something about stupid low-class behavior?

How could she have said such a thing? McCade was sensitive to such put-downs, he always had been. She should have known. And then when she had told him to go to Florida . . .

"Cassandra, I *am* sorry."

"Call me Sandy," she said absently, staring out the window. "I'm not Cassandra, I'm Sandy. I always have been, and it's stupid to try to change this late in the game. *When* are we going to get there?"

The live report from inside the mayor's house was finished but McCade continued shooting the crowd. The station wanted him to scan for local celebrities.

A rock-and-roll band was up on the stage in the big ballroom, turned up so loud it was impossible to talk,

damn near impossible to think. But that was good. Mc-
Cade didn't want to think.

Another ten minutes and he'd help load up the truck,
and the TV crew would be on their way.

His Harley was back at the television station. He'd
originally intended to leave directly from this gig, but
the news editor had told him he'd have a hell of a time
parking. The mayor had recently received an anony-
mous death threat, and while he didn't want to cancel
the party, extra security measures were being taken. No
vehicles were being parked within a two-block radius of
the house, and no one was getting in without an invitation.

McCade's invitation was the video camera he held on
his shoulder. He made one more slow circuit of the
crowd, slowly moving his lens back to the door, adjusting the focus, tightening the frame—

It *was* Sandy. And she was with James Vandenberg.

McCade stood frozen in place, stunned.

They were glancing around the room. As he
watched, Vandenberg put his hand on Sandy's arm. She
turned and looked up into his eyes.

McCade wanted to die. Vandenberg and Sandy were
standing close enough to embrace, close enough to kiss.
Lord, she was wearing her white dress and she looked
beautiful. She said something and Vandenberg reached
out and gripped her shoulders, leaning in close to speak
directly into her ear.

Sandy nodded and smiled up at Vandenberg and Mc-
Cade's heart broke. He'd been gone less than a week, yet
she'd apparently recovered. Hell, she'd obviously done
more than recover. And James hadn't wasted any time
moving into McCade's territory, either.

This was what McCade had wanted.

He shut off his camera and carried it out the back door to the equipment van, moving automatically, going through the motions.

This was what he'd wanted.

He climbed into the back of the van. Someone was in a hurry—the vehicle rolled out of the driveway even before he had a chance to secure his gear.

"Let's see what you got." The news reporter smiled apologetically. "I'm doing the report for tomorrow's broadcast, and I'd like to be out of the editing room before midnight. It's my anniversary."

McCade watched in silence as the reporter rewound and then played back his footage of the party-goers right there on the equipment in the van. She froze the frame on Vandenberg and Sandy. "Isn't that Simon Harcourt's aide?" she asked. "Oh, darn, what's his name?"

"Vandenberg." McCade's eyes were drawn to the video monitor despite his resolve to look away. "James Vandenberg." Just saying the man's name made his teeth hurt. But hey, this *was* what he'd wanted. Sandy's happiness. Right?

The reporter let the tape roll.

On the monitor, Sandy was glancing around the room. She looked up at Vandenberg, then stepped closer to him. They talked, Vandenberg pulled her even closer, she smiled, and the tape was over.

The reporter sat back, making notes on a pad, while McCade stared at the blank screen. What had he just seen? A woman out on the town with her new lover? Something wasn't right, something didn't fit.

"Mind if I rewind and look at it again?" he asked.

The reporter didn't look up from her pad as she gestured toward the equipment. "Be my guest."

McCade slid into the seat directly in front of the

portable editing board and hit rewind. He restarted the tape when James and Sandy walked in. His camera had picked them up even before he'd noticed them.

James gave his invitation to one of the security guards at the door. Sandy spoke to another guard. McCade had been too far away, and the band had been too loud, to hear a word. But he could see her mouth very clearly.

He couldn't read lips if his life depended on it, but it sure as hell looked as if she'd said his name. Clint McCade.

He rewound the tape, tightening the frame of the shot in to a close-up of her face.

Where. The first word she said sure looked like "where." And the very last words were definitely "Clint McCade."

McCade couldn't breathe. Why would Sandy be looking for him while she was out on a date with Vandenberg? Unless . . .

As he watched the monitor Sandy pushed her hair back from her face. Light reflected crazily from her hand.

McCade punched the freeze frame, but her hand was already out of the shot. He quickly rewound, waiting for the flash, and froze the tape.

She was wearing his ring. Lord have mercy, Sandy was wearing the engagement ring he'd bought her. She must have found it in his tuxedo and—

His hands were shaking as he rewound the tape one more time. He readjusted the frame so he could see both Sandy and Vandenberg.

Vandenberg liked her, there was no doubt about that, but his body language wasn't that of a lover. Even when he touched her arm, her shoulders, his grasp was friendly, not intimate. And Sandy—from her body language, McCade could see now that she was impatient and upset. She stepped closer to James Vandenberg only after she frowned slightly and gestured to her ear. She couldn't hear him. He had probably spoken into her ear in order to be heard over the pounding rock and roll, not because he was whispering sweet nothings. And when she smiled at Vandenberg, McCade could see now that it was a smile of gratitude, of thanks.

He rewound the tape and watched it again and again, amazed at how inaccurately he'd read their body language when he'd first caught sight of them.

Sandy had probably come to the party with James because he was the one person she knew who had an invitation. She'd come looking for McCade. She'd come wearing McCade's favorite dress, wearing McCade's diamond ring. Her message was obvious. She'd accepted his marriage proposal—even though he hadn't had the guts to ask. Despite what he thought was best for her, she wanted him. And she wanted him forever, the same way he wanted her. And he *did* want her. Desperately.

She'd come to the mayor's birthday party looking for him, to give him that message, and what had he done?

He had left the building.

He felt a lurch as the van went over the speed bumps in the TV-station parking lot. He had the door opened and was out almost before they were parked.

"Hey, McCade!" the van's driver called after him. "Good luck down in Florida. Drive carefully tonight."

Halfway to his motorcycle McCade stopped, turning back. "I'm not going to Florida tonight." He smiled for what seemed like the first time in days. "I'm going home."

❖━━━━━━━━❖

Sandy was exhausted. There was nothing quite like failure to wear a person out.

She and James had missed McCade by a matter of minutes at the mayor's party, but they'd found out that Frank had been wrong, that McCade had left his motorcycle at the television studio. Sandy called the studio, asking them to give McCade the message to wait, not to leave before he talked to her, while James tried to find out where the parking attendants had stashed his car. They'd had to wait nearly twenty-five minutes, and then they rushed across town, over to the Channel Eight building.

But McCade was gone. He hadn't gone inside, the message Sandy left had never been delivered.

Sandy refused to cry. It was a disappointment, sure, but it was just temporary. After all, it wasn't as if she didn't know where McCade was going. She calculated that if he took his time, he'd need about four days to get to Florida by motorcycle.

It was after midnight by the time she unlocked her apartment door, but she went straight to the telephone and bought herself a one-way plane ticket to Miami. The flight would arrive early Monday afternoon. A second call reserved a rental car.

Then she called Frank. He answered groggily.

"Are you awake?" she asked. "It's me . . . *Sandy.*"

"Yeah." He was instantly alert. "Boss? What's the matter? Is there a problem at the studio?"

"As of Monday, I'm taking a month off," she said. "Give or take a week. And I'm leaving you in charge. Think you can handle it?"

Frank sputtered. "Yeah," he finally managed to say.

"Boy, I must be dreaming. You gonna give me a raise too?"

"Why not? We'll talk more about this tomorrow. Sorry I woke you."

"I'm sure as hell not." Frank laughed. "You won't regret this, boss."

"Yeah," Sandy said. "I know."

She hung up the phone and looked at the clock. Twelve-thirty. It was too late to call Graham Parks to see if he needed any extra help on his shoot. She'd call him first thing in the morning and—

The doorbell rang.

She looked at the clock again, wondering if she'd maybe been wrong about the time. But no, it was definitely half-past midnight.

She knew only one person who would dare to ring her doorbell that late at night. Sandy slowly walked to the door, telling herself not to hope, but hoping anyway. She took a deep breath and looked out of the peephole.

McCade.

She leaned against the door, weak with relief. It was McCade.

Stay calm, she thought, be cool. She had to play it cool. She took a deep breath and opened the door.

McCade looked tired. As tired as she felt.

"I guess you got the message I left at the station after all," she said carefully.

He stepped inside.

Sandy had forgotten how tall he was, how big. He seemed to fill her tiny entryway as he turned to look at her.

"You might say that I got a message of sorts."

His eyes were somber and she wished that he would

smile. He was carrying . . . he was carrying a pair of fishing poles? She looked at him questioningly.

"Some things are worth trying again," he told her quietly. "I figure if you're giving me a second chance, I'll do the same for fishing."

Their eyes met and she wasn't sure who made the first move, but it took just a fraction of a second for her to fall into his arms. He kissed her hard, and she heard a clattering sound—the fishing rods falling to the floor.

McCade was dizzy with relief and emotion as Sandy returned his kisses hungrily. She still wanted him. Thank the Lord, she really did still love him! He kissed her lips, her face, pulling her in close, holding her as if he would never let go. And he wouldn't. Only a damn fool would make a mistake like that twice.

"What makes you so sure I'm going to give you a second chance, McCade?" Sandy murmured before she took his earlobe between her teeth.

He laughed. Lord have mercy, how could he have thought he could live without her? "If I wasn't positive before, I sure as hell am now. Unless you kiss all the suitors you intend to spurn this way?"

But then he lifted her hand so the diamond reflected the light. "To tell you the truth, this ring on your finger was a major hint. This has got to be one of the few times in history an answer to a marriage proposal's been given before the question was asked."

She smiled back at him, amazed at how good she felt. Was it just minutes ago that she'd been so woefully unhappy? "I guess I tipped my hand," she said. "No wonder you seemed so sure of yourself."

McCade's smile faded. "Truth is, the only thing I'm sure about is how much I love you and want you. Do you really think I can give you everything you need?" he asked, his voice low and intense.

Sandy didn't hesitate. "Yes."

A look of wonder softened his somber expression. "You're that certain?" he whispered.

"I've never been more certain of anything in my life," she said. She took a deep breath. "I don't expect you to stop working, and I won't be able to come with you when you go on location, at least not all the time, but—"

"That's the easy part," McCade interrupted. "My job, your job, we can work that out." He stopped, looking down at the floor before he met her eyes again. "It's just that . . . you need to know that I'm never going to be high society, Sandy. I don't have that kind of class or style—"

"You have more class than any man I've ever met," she said indignantly.

"Even when I haul off and hit some lowlife like Aaron Fields in the snout?"

"Well . . ." She smiled. "Nobody's perfect."

"I'm less perfect than most," McCade admitted.

"I'm not perfect either," Sandy told him. "At least *you* didn't break Fields's nose."

He stared at her, trying to decipher her words, then his eyes narrowed as a possible meaning occurred to him. "Are you actually trying to tell me that *you*—"

Sandy nodded. "Three years ago," she said. "He asked me out for dinner, remember?"

"Yeah. You told me. He thought buying you dinner bought him a whole hell of a lot more than your company for the evening."

She stepped away, leaning back against the wall and crossing her arms, as if trying to block the memory.

"Well, he was pretty damn persistent. He wouldn't back off, and I was starting to feel threatened, so I, um, hit him in the face, you know, the way you taught me to."

"With the heel of your hand."

"Exactly." She rolled her eyes. "What a mess."

"The bastard deserved it. Damn, if I had known, I would have hit him harder." McCade tried unsuccessfully to hide a laugh.

Sandy glared at him. "It's not funny, Clint. I thought he was going to throw you in jail—just to get back at me."

He gently massaged her shoulders. "A night in jail wouldn't have killed me. It's not like it hasn't happened before."

She looked up at him, totally shocked.

McCade sighed. "I live in a different world from you, Sandy. You've escaped from my world, and you've forgotten what it's like to live there. My world has people living in the street and lots of pollution and school systems deteriorating because the poor can't afford to pay taxes and the wealthy won't and—" He shook his head. "I've seen too much to ever really leave it behind," he continued. "I guess what I'm trying to say is that I'm a working-class man at heart."

"So?"

He blinked. "So I know what's important to you," he said. "I know you want to join the country club and—"

"Says *who?*" Sandy was staring at him as if he had lost his mind.

"You did," he said with certainty.

"I did not!" she countered indignantly.

"You did too. Back in seventh grade."

She started to laugh. "In seventh grade I *also* wanted to join the air force," she reminded him. "And don't forget that plan I had to train the dogs in the neighbor-hood and go on the road with a canine circus." She smiled at McCade, her eyes dancing with delight. "Are you forgetting the fight I had with my mother because I wanted to get a crew cut and dye the ends of my hair blue? Believe me, I don't want *any* of those things any-more. I want *you.*"

McCade pulled her roughly to him and kissed her again. "I love you." He pulled back and looked search-ingly at her. "I don't want you to make a mistake that you'll regret."

"I could say the same thing to you." Her face was suddenly serious. "Are you sure you're ready to settle down, commit to one person?"

"I want to buy a house with you," he said, running his fingers through her long, golden hair. "A big house with a yard—a big yard, a few acres at least. I want to get some horses and a big dog, and then maybe in a few years, a pony or two for the kids—"

"Kids," Sandy repeated faintly.

"I want you too," he said, cupping her face with his hands and kissing her. "I want you beside me for the rest of my life, Sandy. I want to wear a ring on my finger that tells the world you own my heart. I want to make babies with you, lots of babies with your beautiful eyes—"

"And your smile," she whispered. "I hope they have your smile, Clint."

He slowly dropped to one knee. "Marry me, Sandy."

"I already gave you my answer," she said softly.

"I want to hear you say it. I want to do this right."

His hair had fallen across his forehead, and he pushed it back impatiently as he gazed at her. She was going to remember this forever, Sandy realized, looking down into his familiar, handsome face. He was wearing a red T-shirt with his jeans tonight. The shirt had shrunk from repeated washings, and the faded cotton stretched across his broad shoulders and chest. Yes, she was definitely going to remember this moment for the rest of her life.

"Yes," she told him softly. "I'll marry you."

He smiled as he looked up at her and she could see happiness in his eyes, happiness and contentment and a deep, inner peace.

"Good," he said, more to himself than to her. "That's really good."

McCade stood up then and kissed her, a slow, sweet kiss that made her tremble. He picked her up, cradling her in his arms and started down the hallway toward her bedroom. Halfway there he stopped, swearing softly. "I've got to go to Florida. I made Parks a commitment, and I can't get out of it now."

She pulled his head down, kissing him again. "You don't need to go tonight. Do you?"

Although he was seriously distracted by her lips, he managed to pull away long enough to say, "I'm supposed to be there Tuesday morning. If I'm taking my bike—" She kissed him longer and deeper and he groaned. "I don't want to go—"

"Leave your motorcycle here," Sandy murmured, trailing kisses along his jawline to his neck. "You can take a plane to Florida. There're still empty seats on a flight that leaves Monday. That's when I'm going."

She kissed him on the mouth again, and he responded with passion until her words sank in.

McCade set Sandy down on the floor and stared at her. "That's when you're what?"

"Going." She smiled. "To Florida. To be with you."

She loved him. She loved him enough to follow him

across the country. She'd booked that flight even though he'd walked out on her, even though he'd pretended that he didn't want her anymore. He'd done all that, hurt her badly, and she'd still managed to see through him, to see how he truly felt. And all this time he'd thought *he* was the expert on body language.

She gently touched his cheek. "I love you."

"Marry me tomorrow," McCade said huskily. "We can drive up to Vegas, and—"

"Can we wait till we get to Florida?" Sandy asked. "Then my mother can be at our wedding. I know she'd like that. She's going to be so excited."

He frowned. "You sure she's forgiven me for that fishhook in your foot?"

"If she hasn't, just whisper the word 'grandchildren' and see how quickly she warms up to you."

He smiled. Then frowned again. "Why the *hell* are we standing here talking?"

"For a man who knows so much about body language, you *do* tend to spend an awful lot of time talking," she teased.

McCade lifted her up and took her into her bedroom. Then, without saying another word, he told her quite clearly how much he loved her.

THE EDITORS' CORNER

To celebrate our fifteenth anniversary, we have decided to couple this month with a very special theme. For many, the paranormal has always been intriguing, whether it's mystical convergences, the space-time continuum, the existence of aliens, or speculation about the afterlife. We went to our own LOVESWEPT authors and asked them to come up with their most intriguing ideas. And thus the EXTRAORDINARY LOVERS theme month was born. Have fun with this taste of the supernatural, but first check beneath the bed, then snuggle under the covers. And don't let the bedbugs bite . . . they do exist, you know!

Brianne St. John is finding herself **NEVER ALONE,** in Cheryln Biggs's LOVESWEPT #890. It's hard enough when just one ghost is hanging around, but what does a girl do when four insistent ghosts are on her case? Ever since she was a little girl, she's had Athos, Porthos, Aramis, and yes, even D'Artagnan to scare all her boyfriends away. Now that gorgeous entrepreneur Mace Calder has set foot in Leimonte Castle, the four musketeers are in an uproar! Mace has noticed that the lady of the house tends to mutter to herself a great deal, but for now he has other important matters to take care of. As Mace and Brianne draw closer, strange things keep happening, objects are being moved, shadows are darkening doorways—and Mace wonders just when is that wall going to answer Brianne? Cheryln Biggs revisits old haunts and legends in this enchanting romp of a love story!

Journalist Nate Wagner has his hands full when he confronts **WITCHY WOMAN** Tess DeWitt, in LOVESWEPT #891 by Karen Leabo. What strikes Nate about the beautiful woman he's followed into a Back Bay antique shop is that she doesn't look like the notorious Moonbeam Majick, a witch who disappeared fifteen years ago. Tess knew she and everyone around her were in harm's way the minute she came across the cursed cat statue that had very nearly ruined her life. Teamed up with an insatiably curious Nate, Tess must find a way to save her best friend's life, prevent Nate from dying, and keep the cat away from the mysterious stranger who's bent on unleashing the statue's unholy powers. In the end, will a spell cast from loving hearts be enough to save them all from certain death? Karen Leabo delves into the mystical connections our souls offer to those we truly love.

Loveswept veteran Peggy Webb gives us **NIGHT OF THE DRAGON**, LOVESWEPT #892. With only a book and an ancient ring to guide her, Lydia

Star falls back in time and lands at the feet of a fire-breathing dragon. Lydia is saved by one of King Arthur's brave knights, Sir Dragon, and is forced to face the fact that she's not in San Diego anymore. Dragon is bewildered by his mysterious prisoner, but can't help being captivated by her ethereal beauty. Convinced that she is the result of some deviltry, he confides in the king's counsel, Merlyn. Lydia knows her time is running out and longs for the comforts of home, a fact that keeps her trying desperately to escape from the overbearing knight's clutches. Can this warrior be the keeper of her soul? Better yet, will he survive the journey to his heart's true home? Peggy Webb more than answers these questions with this sensual dream of a romance.

Catherine Mulvany treats us to **AQUAMARINE**, LOVESWEPT #893. Teague Harris can't believe his eyes when he sees his supposedly dead fiancée walking around the carnival grounds. He's even more surprised when he realizes that Shea McKenzie might not be his former love . . . but she does look enough like Kirsten Rainey to pose as the missing heiress for Kirsten's dying father. Drawn to Idaho by a postcard found among her dead mother's things, Shea reluctantly agrees to the outrageous masquerade after seeing a picture of a man who could pass for her own father. Then, as Shea discovers a cluster of glowing aquamarine crystals, she begins to experience Kirsten's memories. Can Shea trust Teague, a man who seems more interested in trying to solve the murder of Shea's twin than in moving on with the rest of his life? Catherine Mulvany teaches us that love is the strongest force on earth!

Happy reading!

With warmest wishes,

Susann Brailey Joy Abella

Susann Brailey   Joy Abella

Senior Editor   Administrative Editor

P.S. Look for these women's fiction titles coming in June! From Nora Roberts comes **GENUINE LIES**, now in hardcover for the first time ever. Hollywood legend Eve Benedict selects Julia Summers to write her biography. Sparks fly and danger looms as three Hollywood players attempt to protect what they value most. Talented author Jane Feather introduces an irresistible new trilogy, beginning with **THE HOSTAGE BRIDE.** Three girls make a pact never to get married, but when Portia is accidentally kidnapped by a gang of outlaws, her hijacker gets more than he bargained for in his defiant and surprisingly attractive captive. And finally, Rebecca Kelley presents her debut, **THE WEDDING CHASE.** Zel Fleetwood is looking for a wealthy husband who can save her family. Instead she attracts the unwanted attentions of the earl of Northcliffe, whose ardent but misguided interest ruins her prospects. That is, until he realizes *he*'s the perfect match for her. And immediately following this page, preview the Bantam women's fiction titles on sale in May!

For current information on Bantam's women's fiction, visit our Web site at the following address:
http://www.bdd.com/romance

Don't miss these extraordinary
novels from Bantam Books!

On sale in May:

A PLACE TO
CALL HOME
by Deborah Smith

THE WITCH AND
THE WARRIOR
by Karyn Monk

Come home to the best-loved novel
of the year . . .

A Place to Call Home
BY DEBORAH SMITH

*Twenty years ago, Claire Maloney was the willful, pampered,
tomboyish daughter of the town's most respected family, but
that didn't stop her from befriending Roan Sullivan, a fierce,
motherless boy who lived in a rusted-out trailer amid junked
cars. No one in Dunderry, Georgia—least of all Claire's family—could understand the bond between these two mavericks.
But Roan and Claire belonged together . . . until the dark
afternoon when violence and terror overtook them, and Roan
disappeared from Claire's life. Now, two decades later, Claire
is adrift, and the Maloneys are still hoping the past can be
buried under the rich Southern soil. But Roan Sullivan is
about to walk back into their lives. . . . By turns tender and
sexy and heartbreaking and exuberant,* A Place to Call
Home *is an enthralling journey between two hearts—and a
deliciously original novel from one of the most imaginative
and appealing new voices in Southern fiction.*

"A beautiful, believable love story."
—*Chicago Tribune*

It started the year I performed as a tap-dancing leprechaun at the St. Patrick's Day carnival and Roanie Sullivan threatened to cut my cousin Carlton's throat with a
rusty pocketknife. That was also the year the Beatles
broke up and the National Guard killed four students at

Kent State, and Josh, who was in Vietnam, wrote home to Brady, who was a senior at Dunderry High, *Don't even think about enlisting. There's nothing patriotic about this shit.*

But I was only five years old; my world was narrow, deep, self-satisfied, well-off, very Southern, securely bound to the land and to a huge family descended almost entirely from Irish immigrants who had settled in the Georgia mountains over one hundred and thirty years ago. As far as I was concerned, life revolved in simple circles with me at the center.

The St. Patrick's Day carnival was nothing like it is now. There were no tents set up to dispense green beer, no artists selling handmade 24-karat-gold shamrock jewelry, no Luck of the Irish 5K Road Race, no imported musicians playing authentic Irish jigs on the town square. Now it's a *festival*, one of the top tourist events in the state.

But when I was five it was just a carnival, held in the old Methodist campground arbor east of town. The Jaycees and the Dunderry Ladies' Association sold barbecue sandwiches, green sugar cookes, and lime punch at folding tables in a corner next to the arbor's wooden stage, the Down Mountain Boys played bluegrass music, and the beginners' tap class from my Aunt Gloria's School of Dance was decked out in leprechaun costumes and forced into a mid-year minirecital.

Mama took snapshots of me in my involuntary servitude. I was not a born dancer. I had no rhythm, I was always out of step, and I disliked mastering anyone's routines but my own. I stood there on the stage, staring resolutely at the camera in my green-checkered bibbed dress with its ruffled skirt and a puffy white blouse, my green socks and black patent-leather tap shoes with green bows, my hair parted in fat red braids tied with green ribbons.

I looked like an unhappy Irish Heidi.

My class, all twenty of us, stomped and shuffled through our last number, accompanied by a tune from some Irish dance record I don't remember, which Aunt Gloria played full blast on her portable stereo connected to the Down Mountain Boys' big amplifiers. I looked down and there he was, standing in the crowd at the lip of the stage, a tall, shabby, ten-year-old boy with greasy black hair. Roan Sullivan. *Roanie.* Even in a small town the levels of society are a steep staircase. My family was at the top. Roan and his daddy weren't just at the bottom; they were in the cellar.

He watched me seriously, as if I weren't making a fool of myself, which I was. I had already accidentally stomped on my cousin Violet's left foot twice, and I'd elbowed my cousin Rebecca in her right arm, so they'd given me a wide berth on either side.

I forgot about my humiliating arms and feet and concentrated on Roanie Sullivan avidly, because it was the first close look I'd gotten at nasty, no-account Big Roan Sullivan's son from Sullivan's Hollow. We didn't associate with Big Roan Sullivan, even though he and Roanie were our closest neighbors on Soap Falls Road. The Hollow might as well have been on the far side of China, not two miles from our farm.

"That godforsaken hole only produces one thing— *trash.*" That's what Uncle Pete and Uncle Bert always said about the Hollow. And because everybody knew Roanie Sullivan was trash—came from it, looked like it, and smelled like it—they steered clear of him in the crowd. Maybe that was one reason I couldn't take my eyes off him. We were both human islands stuck in the middle of a lonely, embarrassing sea of space.

My cousin Carlton lounged a couple of feet away, between Roanie and the Jaycees' table. There are some relatives you just tolerate, and Carlton Maloney was in that group. He was about twelve, smug and well-fed, and he was laughing at me so hard that his eyes nearly disappeared in his face. He and my brother Hop were in the seventh grade together. Hop said he cheated on math tests. He was a weasel.

I saw him glance behind him. Once, twice. Uncle Dwayne was in charge of the Jaycees' food table and Aunt Rhonda was talking to him about something, so he was looking at her dutifully. He'd left a couple of dollar bills beside the cardboard shoe box he was using as a cash till.

Carlton eased one hand over, snatched the money, and stuck it in his trouser pocket.

I was stunned. He'd stolen from the Jaycees. He'd stolen from his own *uncle*. My brothers and I had been trained to such a strict code of honor that we wouldn't pilfer so much as a penny from the change cup on Daddy's dresser. I admit I had a weakness for the bags of chocolate chips in the bakery section of the grocery store, and if one just *happened* to fall off the shelf and burst open, I'd sample a few. But nonedible property was sacred. And stealing *money* was unthinkable.

Uncle Dwayne looked down at the table. He frowned. He hunted among packages of sugar cookies wrapped in cellophane and tied with green ribbons. He leaned toward Carlton and said something to him. From the stage I couldn't hear what he said—I couldn't hear anything except the music pounding in my ears—but I saw Carlton draw back dramatically, shaking his head. Then he turned and pointed at Roanie.

I was struck tapless. I simply couldn't move a foot. I stood there, rooted in place, and was dimly, painfully aware of people laughing at me, of my grandparents hiding their smiles behind their hands, and of Mama's and

Daddy's bewildered stares. Daddy, who could not dance either, waved his big hands helpfully, as if I was a scared calf he could shoo into moving again.

But I wasn't scared. I was furious.

Uncle Dwayne, his jaw thrust out, pushed his way around the table and grabbed Roanie by one arm. I saw Uncle Dwayne speak forcefully to him. I saw the blank expression on Roanie's face turn to sullen anger. I guess it wasn't the first time he'd been accused of something he didn't do.

His eyes darted to Carlton. He lunged at him. They went down in a heap, with Carlton on the bottom. People scattered, yelling. The whole Leprechaun Review came to a wobbly halt. Aunt Gloria bounded to her portable record player and the music ended with a screech like an amplified zipper. I bolted down the stairs at that end of the stage and squirmed through the crowd of adults.

Uncle Dwayne was trying to pull Roanie off Carlton, but Roanie had one hand wound in the collar of Carlton's sweater. He had the other at Carlton's throat, with the point of a rusty little penknife poised beneath Carlton's Adam's apple. "I didn't take no money!" Roanie yelled at him. "You damn liar!"

Daddy plowed into the action. He planted a knee in Roanie's back and wrenched the knife out of his hand. He and Uncle Dwayne pried the boys apart, and Daddy pulled Roanie to his feet. "He has a knife," I heard someone whisper. "That Sullivan boy's vicious."

"Where's that money?" Uncle Dwayne thundered, peering down into Roanie Sullivan's face. "Give it to me. Right now."

"I ain't got no money. I didn't take no money." He mouthed words like a hillbilly, kind of honking them out half finished. He had a crooked front tooth with jagged edges, too. It flashed like a lopsided fang.

"Oh, yeah, you did," Carlton yelled. "I saw you! Everybody knows you steal stuff! Just like your daddy!"

"Roanie, hand over the money," Daddy said. Daddy had a booming voice. He was fair, but he was tough. "Don't make me go through your pockets," he added sternly. "Come on, boy, tell the truth and give the money back."

"I ain't *got* it."

I was plastered to the sidelines but close enough to see the misery and defensiveness in Roanie's face. Oh, lord. He was the kind of boy who fought and cussed and put a knife to people's throats. He caused trouble. He deserved trouble.

But he's not a thief.

Don't tattle on Carlton. Maloneys stick together. We're big, that way.

But it's not fair.

"All right, Roanie," Daddy said, and reached for the back pocket of Roanie's dirty jeans.

"He didn't take it," I said loudly. "Carlton did!" Everyone stared at me. Well, I'd gotten used to that. I met Roanie Sullivan's wary, surprised eyes. He could burn a hole through me with those eyes.

Uncle Dwayne glared at me. "Now, Claire. Are you sure you're not getting back at Carlton because he spit boiled peanuts at you outside Sunday school last week?"

No, but I knew how a boiled peanut felt. Hot, real hot. "Roanie didn't take the money," I repeated. I jabbed a finger at Carlton. "Carlton did. I *saw* him, Daddy. I saw him stick it in his front pocket."

Daddy and Uncle Dwayne pivoted slowly. Carlton's face, already sweaty and red, turned crimson. "*Carlton,*" Uncle Dwayne said.

"She's just picking on me!"

Uncle Dwayne stuck a hand in Carlton's pocket and pulled out two wadded-up dollar bills.

And that was that.

Uncle Dwayne hauled Carlton off to find Uncle Eugene and Aunt Arnetta, Carlton's folks. Daddy let go of Roanie Sullivan. "Go on. Get out of here."

"He pulled that knife, Holt," Uncle Pete said behind me.

Daddy scowled. "He couldn't cut his way out of a paper sack with a knife that little."

"But he *pulled* it on Carlton."

"Forget about it, Pete. Go on, everybody."

Roanie stared at me. I held his gaze as if hypnotized. Isolation radiated from him like an invisible shield, but there was this *gleam* in his eyes, made up of surprise and gratitude and suspicion, bearing on me like concentrated fire, and I felt singed. Daddy put a hand on the collar of the faded, floppy football jersey he wore and dragged him away. I started to follow, but Mama had gotten through the crowd by then, and she snagged me by the back of my dress. "Hold on, Claire Karleen Maloney. You've put on enough of a show."

Dazed, I looked up at her. Hop and Evan peered at me from her side. Violet and Rebecca watched me, open-mouthed. A whole bunch of Maloneys scrutinized me. "Carlton's a weasel," I explained finally.

Mama nodded. "You told the truth. That's fine. You're done. I'm proud of you."

"Then how come everybody's lookin' at me like I'm weird?"

"Because you *are*," Rebecca blurted out. "Aren't you scared of Roanie Sullivan?"

"He didn't laugh at me when I was dancing. I think he's okay."

"You've got a strange way of sortin' things out," Evan said.

"She's one brick short of a load," Hop added.

So that was the year I realized Roanie was not just trashy, not just different, he was dangerous, and taking his side was a surefire way to seed my own mild reputation as a troublemaker and Independent Thinker.

I was fascinated by him from then on.

"An enthralling tale of two compelling, heartwarming characters and the healing power of love . . . I loved it!"—Elizabeth Thornton, author of *You Only Love Twice*

The historical tales of Karyn Monk are filled with unforgettable romance and her own special brand of warmth and humor. Now love casts its spell in the Highlands, as a warrior seeks a miracle from a mysterious lady of secrets and magic. . . .

The Witch and the Warrior
BY KARYN MONK

Suspected of witchcraft, Gwendolyn MacSween has been condemned to being burned at the stake at the hands of her own clan. Yet rescue comes from a most unlikely source. Mad Alex MacDunn, laird of the mighty rival clan MacDunn, is a man whose past is scarred with tragedy and loss. His last hope lies in capturing the witch of the MacSweens—and using her magic to heal his dying son. He expects to find an old hag. . . . Instead he finds a young woman of unearthly beauty. There's only one problem: Gwendolyn has no power to bewitch or to heal. Now she must pretend to be a sorceress—or herself perish. But can she use her common sense to save Alex's son, and her natural powers as a woman to enchant a fierce and handsome Highland warrior—before a dangerous enemy destroys them both?

Gwendolyn regarded the sky in bewilderment. She had never witnessed such an abrupt change in the weather.

"Everything is fine," she assured them loudly. "The spirits have heard my plea."

They remained in their circle, watching the sky as a cool gale whipped their hair and clothes. And then, just as suddenly as it burst upon them, the storm died. The wind gasped and was gone, and the clouds melted into the darkness, unveiling the silent, tranquil glow of the moon and stars once again.

"By God, that was something!" roared Cameron, slapping Brodick heartily on the back. "Have you ever seen such a thing?"

"Did you see that, Alex?" demanded Brodick, looking uneasy.

"Aye," said Alex. "I saw."

Brodick raised his arm and cautiously flexed it at the elbow. "I think my arm feels better." He sounded more troubled than pleased.

"I *know* my head feels better!" said Cameron happily. "What about you, Neddie?"

"I have no wounds for the witch to heal," said Ned, shrugging. He frowned, then shrugged again. "That's odd," he remarked, slowly turning his head from side to side. "My neck has been stiff and aching for a week, and suddenly it feels fine."

Gwendolyn folded her arms across her chest and regarded them triumphantly. Clearly just the suggestion that they would feel better had had an effect on them, which was what she had hoped would happen. Luckily, the weather had complemented her little performance.

"Can you cast that spell on anyone?" asked Cameron, still excited.

"Not everyone," she replied carefully. "And my spells don't always work."

"What do you mean?" demanded Alex.

"The success of a spell depends on many things," she replied evasively. She did not want him to think she could simply say a few words and fell an entire army. "My powers will not work on everyone."

"I don't give a damn if they work on everyone," he growled. "As long as they work on one person." His expression was harsh. "Cameron, take the first watch. The rest of you get some sleep. We ride at first light."

Brodick produced an extra plaid from his horse and carefully draped it over Isabella's unconscious form. Then he lay down just a few feet away from her, where he could watch over her during the night. Ned and MacDunn also stretched out upon the ground, arranging part of their plaids over their shoulders for warmth.

"Do you sleep standing up?" MacDunn asked irritably.

"No," replied Gwendolyn.

"Then lie down," he orderd. "We still have a long journey ahead."

She had assumed they were going to bind her to a tree. But with Cameron watching her, she would not get very far if she attempted to escape tonight. Obviously that was what MacDunn believed. Relieved that she would not be tied, she wearily lowered herself to the ground.

Tomorrow would be soon enough to find an opportunity for escape.

The little camp grew quiet, except for the occasional snap of the fire. Soon the rumble of snoring began to drift lazily through the air. Gwendolyn wondered how they had all managed to find sleep so quickly in such uncomfortable conditions. The fire had died and the ground was damp and cold, forcing her to curl into a tight ball and wrap her bare arms around herself. It didn't help. With every passing moment her flesh grew more chilled, until finally her entire body was shivering uncontrollably.

"Gwendolyn," called MacDunn in a low voice, "come here."

She sat up and peered at him through the darkness. "Why?" she demanded suspiciously.

"Because your chattering teeth are keeping me awake," he grumbled. "You will lie next to me and share my plaid."

She stared at him in horror. "I am fine, MacDunn," she hastily assured him. "You needn't concern yourself about—"

"Come here," he repeated firmly.

"No," she replied, shaking her head. "I may be your prisoner, but I will *not* share your bed."

She waited for him to argue. Instead he muttered something under his breath, adjusted his plaid more to his liking over his naked chest and closed his eyes once again. Satisfied that she had won this small but critical battle, she vigorously rubbed her arms to warm them, then primly curled onto the ground.

Her teeth began to chatter so violently she had to bite down hard to try to control them.

The next thing she knew, MacDunn was stretching out beside her and wrapping his plaid over both of them.

"Don't you dare touch me!" Gwendolyn hissed, rolling away.

MacDunn grabbed her waist and firmly drew her back, imprisoning her in the warm crook of his enormous, barely clad body.

"Be still!" he ordered impatiently.

"I will not be still, you foul, mad ravisher of women!" She kicked him as hard as she could in his shin.

"Jesus—" he swore, loosening his hold slightly.

Gwendolyn tried to scramble away from him, but he instantly tightened his grip.

"Listen to me!" he commanded, somehow managing to keep his voice low. "I have no intention of bedding you, do you understand?"

Gwendolyn glared at him, her breasts rising and falling so rapidly they grazed his bandaged chest.

"I may be considered mad," he continued, "but to my knowledge I have not yet earned a reputation as a ravager of unwilling women—do you understand?"

His blue eyes held hers. She tried to detect deceit in them, but could not. All she saw was anger, mingled with weariness.

"I have already risked far more than I have a right to, to save your life and take you home with me, Gwendolyn MacSween," he continued. "I will *not* have it end by watching you fall deathly ill from the chill of the night."

He waited a moment, allowing his comments to penetrate her fear. Then, cautiously, he loosened his grip. "Lie still," he ordered gruffly. "I will keep you warm, nothing more. You have my word."

She regarded him warily. "You swear you will not abuse me, MacDunn? On your honor?"

"I swear."

Reluctantly, she eased herself onto her side. MacDunn adjusted part of his plaid over her, then once again fitted himself around her. His arm circled her waist, drawing her into the warm, hard cradle of his body. Gwendolyn lay there rigidly for a long while, scarcely breathing, waiting for him to break his word.

Instead, he began to snore.

Heat seemed to radiate from him, slowly permeating

her chilled flesh. It warmed even the soft wool of his plaid, she realized, snuggling further into it. A deliciously masculine scent wafted around her, the scent of horse and leather and woods. Little by little, the feel of MacDunn's powerful body against hers became more comforting than threatening, especially as his snores grew louder.

Until that moment, she had had virtually no knowledge of physical contact. Her mother had died when she was very young, and her father, though loving, had never been at ease with open demonstrations of affection. The unfamiliar sensation of MacDunn's warm body wrapped protectively around her was unlike anything she had ever imagined. She was his prisoner. And yet, she felt impossibly safe.

"You belong to me now," he had told her. *"I protect what is mine."* She belonged to no one. She reflected drowsily, and no one could protect her from men like Robert, or the ignorance and fear that was sure to fester in MacDunn's own clan the moment they saw her. She would escape him long before they reached his lands. Tomorrow, she would break free from these warriors, so she could retrieve the stone, return to her clan and kill Robert. Above all else, Robert must die. She would make him pay for murdering her father and destroying her life.

But all this seemed distant and shadowy as she drifted into slumber, sheltered by this brave, mad warrior, whose heart pulsed steadily against her back.

On sale in June:

GENUINE LIES
by Nora Roberts

THE HOSTAGE BRIDE
by Jane Feather

THE WEDDING CHASE
by Rebecca Kelley